Dr. Wren's INCREDIBLE Hoverpark of WONDER

SHELLY DRUMMOND

BRUTON MEMORIAL LIBRARY
302 McLENDON STREET
PLANT CITY, FLORIDA 33563

Copyright © 2015 Shelly Drummond.

All rights reserved. No part of this book may be reproduced, stored, or transmitted by any means—whether auditory, graphic, mechanical, or electronic—without written permission of both publisher and author, except in the case of brief excerpts used in critical articles and reviews. Unauthorized reproduction of any part of this work is illegal and is punishable by law.

Dr. Wren's Incredible Hoverpark of Wonder is a work of fiction and all places and characters in the book are entirely fictional. Any similarity to actual people or places is purely coincidental.

ISBN: 978-0-9962-1081-2 (sc)
ISBN: 978-0-9962-1080-5 (e)

Because of the dynamic nature of the Internet, any web addresses or links contained in this book may have changed since publication and may no longer be valid. The views expressed in this work are solely those of the author and do not necessarily reflect the views of the publisher, and the publisher hereby disclaims any responsibility for them.

Published by: Thin Husk
P.O. Box 3641
Plant City, FL 33563
813-731-6809

rev. date: 06/11/2015

For Sara Agnes

my daughter and my inspiration

Contents

1. Travis 1
2. Toggles 9
3. Grayson Elementary 16
4. Tampa Docks 27
5. Welcome 36
6. On Maps 49
7. The Vonderheist 60
8. Windy City Woes 70
9. The Centrifuge 78
10. Scheming 89
11. Ma Ridgley's 98
12. Mt. Alta 105
13. Fractured 115
14. Try, Try, Again 121
15. Stuck 129
16. The Wrenaissance Theatre of Wonders 134
17. Surprises 144
18. Trouble in Paradise 151

19.	The GENsys	159
20.	Gravity	168
21.	Intruders	183
22.	Waltz of the Biotags	191
23.	Meanwhile	203
24.	Together	211
25.	Questions	216
26.	Relaxing	224
27.	The Imag'n'ator	232
28.	Lessons	238
29.	Finale	248
30.	Path of Egress	254
31.	Luminous	261
32.	Goodbye	267
33.	Going Home	273

"Live the Wonder"

1

Travis

CLOUDS AND A FIBERGLASS PARROT are melting on the set as an acrid smoke fills the room. An alarm is going off somewhere - everywhere! Bright strobe lights blink to a skipping soundtrack and flames cast shadows against swirling pirates on a ship below, dancing round and round. Flames are licking the walls of the dark ride, the scene is burning and the screams of horrified riders punctuate the music.

Wide eyed and tentative, five year old Travis is walking on a black emergency walkway, hand in hand with his twin sister Tara. Their shoelaces are glowing white in the black light as the twins step carefully alongside the track. In a burning heap, a smiling mannequin suddenly falls across the path between them. Travis pulls back his hand, looks at his sister and looks down at the mannequin. The mannequin's golden hair is engulfed in flames and her bright blue eyes are melting into black. The lights flicker.

In horror he realizes Tara is gone and he is alone. A voice calls out from the other side of the track, the dark side of the carts.

"Travis," His Dad is holding Tara in one hand and reaching out to him with the other. Between them lies a shadowy, smoking chasm that opens into the burning scene below him.

"You have to jump across it Travis!"

Now the ship's sails are on fire and the waves are turning into a foaming black liquid. The walkway he is on is burning and Travis must go between the carts and leap over the track. He coughs in the toxic smoke-there is no time. He steps back and then forward again, leaping with commitment towards the safety of his father. His sister Tara calls out through the smoke, "Travis!"

Startled, he lifts his head just slightly and in doing so he misses his mark. His Dad's hand remains out of reach and Travis tumbles in mid air! He cascades down towards the ship burning in a swirl of plastic rocks, black water and red lights. Travis flails uselessly at a mass of scenic vines, cords and fiberglass branches in a free fall off the sheer wall. Tara's voice breaks through the smoke interrupting again, "Travis!"

With a start he wakes up, eyes open and hyper alert. His heart is pounding. He starts muttering the mantra, "OK, I'm OK, It's OK" until, with a good amount of comfort, he realizes he's at home, in his own bed. A wave of relief rolls over Travis and he hits the snooze button. Lying in the bed, he slowly focuses on the small stain on the ceiling where the roof has started to leak. Almost simultaneously, the alarm goes off again and Tara pounds on the door to his room, "Travis, Get up!"

"I'm up" Travis calls back.

Stamping off the alarm again with his hand, he glanced at his calendar - March 25th. The flash of animated fireworks on the calendar reminded him today was their field trip! Travis leapt out of bed, in a mad dash of enthusiasm. He'd been waiting for this all year. Today - correction - on this particularly gloriously, sunny yet not too hot day, Travis and his twin sister Tara were joining their 5th grade class on a trip to the ultimate theme park - Hoverpark!

Hoverpark was the perfect mix of technology and adrenaline. To begin with, the park floats in mid air over the Gulf of Mexico and only docks in Tampa part of the year. It's a huge theme park, with state of the art thrills, like the Vonderheist (only the best roller coaster in the world!) Even better, the whole park is interactive. Everything you do is part of a game. You can design your own rides, explore the island finding hidden digital keys and there are advanced puzzles for gamers to work. Travis could barely contain his excitement. But first, there were niceties to attend to, fresh socks being a priority.

The top drawer of his dresser was practically empty. A quick search produced one clean sock. Distracted, he scanned the pile of clothes in the corner, grabbed a loose sock, smelled it and quickly wiggled his left foot into it. A fresh sock on his right foot, he now reached for shoes. To the casual observer, Travis Pruitt was almost a typical 11 year old. He was a fan of digital gaming, he liked camping (it was sort of a thing he had going with his Mom) and he didn't like to clean his room.

He had a striking appearance, due to a streak of white running through his shock of red hair. This was just a result of a birthmark, nothing dramatic, though his friend Hank sometimes invented stories for him. Hank once told their second grade teacher that Travis had been hit by a falling bit of space debris. For years his friend Luci thought he'd been bit as a child by a sand shark. Sometimes Travis went along with Hank's stories. He sheepishly learned his lesson at a class party though, when his mother wholeheartedly denied any random contact with a rogue asteroid as well as additional allegations of being carried off by a gator as a baby.

As Travis slipped on his shoes, panic set in, "Where is my belt!?"

By belt, Travis meant his utility belt, made especially for the Hoverpark. It was an over the shoulder bandolier belt, only it was much more functional. It had special eyelets where you could attach your park toggles. You could also use one of the riveted pouches for carting around your teletab or any other supplies or equipment you might need. Wearing the belt and showing off your toggles was one of the best parts of the park, which is why

Travis lost his cool. He'd been waiting for today for months and now he couldn't remember where his belt was! He tore through his drawers and desk. How could he be such an idiot? Frustrated, he ripped opened his closet door only to have a football helmet tumble down on his head. Rubbing a red splotch on his forehead, he stepped back and moaned, "umph."

"Ouch" his twin sister Tara laughed. She was standing in the doorway, hairbrush in hand.

"So, why do you still have that helmet anyway? You hated playing football." She was slight compared to Travis, who looked like he'd be a great football player.

"I don't know," Travis started tossing items out of the closet as he spoke; a fishing rod, an old Lego set, a rain jacket, a backpack and boots.

"I keep thinking it might come in handy. You never know when a bunch of crazed jocks might come charging at you." He grinned at Tara as he flung a box of very old computer parts at the bed, the ribbon cables and cords spilling out like snakes on the carpet.

"Just help me find my toggle belt," Travis insisted, rubbing his head again. "Please."

"You shouldn't have waited 'til the last minute."

Tara rolled her eyes as she tiptoed her way carefully across the mess. Her sharp eyebrows were naturally expressive and she often worked them to her advantage. Opening a drawer in Travis's night table, Tara reached back past empty snack wrappers, cords, tape covered screwdrivers and tiny screws to produce a utility belt, decorated with metal badges. The belt had a large copper colored clasp and a Hoverpark logo. Five glowing badges or toggles were attached to the belt and each animated toggle began moving as the sunlight in the window activated their solar cells. Travis put it on his shoulder and smiled proudly, basking in toggle glory or 'toglory' as he liked to call it.

"Thanks. Really Tara, I can't thank you enough," Travis beamed, then his eyes glanced to the left, "But scoot - I need the bathroom. I'm running late." And he pushed past his protesting twin in a mad dash for the hall bathroom.

"Travis!" Tara pounded on the bathroom door as it slammed shut.

"Can't talk now sis', I'm busy brushing my teeth." Travis turned on the radio to drown out her protests. He carefully opened Tara's makeup drawer, caught the lizard as it leaped out (he had put it there yesterday evening) and slipped it through the hole in the screen window. One good turn deserves another Travis figured. And besides he really did need to brush his teeth.

"Don't forget breakfast!" A groggy, but obviously no-nonsense voice rang out from the downstairs kitchen. Their mother, Penelope Pruitt, was just half way through her first cup of coffee; but she was right on schedule as usual. As a chaperone for today's field trip, coffee and breakfast were a priority. She was an early riser, partially due to the fact that she grew up on a ranch in central Florida. She hadn't been on a horse in 25 years, but her love of jeans lingered. Travis and Tara had resigned themselves to her penchant for 20th century western wear fashion, especially the snap button western shirts, one of which she was obviously planning on wearing to the park today. In cowboy boots, she leaned against the counter watching the news report. "Temperature 78 degrees, chance of rain 10 %, allergy forecast: high for Oak; terror projection: low." It was, as usual, a perfect spring day in Tampa, Florida.

"Travis, Tara- you need to eat breakfast!" Penelope Pruitt insisted. Food is really expensive at the Hoverpark, so today especially, they needed to eat well. Travis made it to the table first.

"Tara is on her way." He smiled.

"Don't be so mean to your sister." His mother cut her eye at him from the sink. "She's the only twin you've got."

"Did you notice I mowed the lawn yesterday?" Travis asked casually between bites off waffle.

His Mom was not easily distracted. "I mean it Travis. You two fight a lot now, but it wasn't always that way. One day it will just be the two of you. You came into this world together and you shouldn't forget that."

"Travis, are you listening?" His mother said.

"Yes Ma'm." Travis smiled. It didn't hurt to practice manners. And he was actually getting a bit anxious.

"That's more like it. Yes, I noticed you've been mowing regularly without being asked…but money is tight, especially with this field trip." Mrs. Pruitt paused for dramatic effect. Travis was visibly nervous but didn't want to ask. Finally she added, "But I managed to save up a little and I put $100 credit in your bio-account. And $100 for you as well, Tara."

Tara had just made it to the table and the news visibly cheered her up. The late bathroom hadn't done her any harm; she was neat and polished as usual. A minimalist by nature, Tara was not one for frills and fop. Her interests didn't include the pony show of preteen fashion. Her only bit of flash was a pair of colorful glasses and very long, beautiful, deep auburn curls.

Obviously not identical, Travis and Tara were fraternal twins. Travis had freckles to begin with; big red ones across his nose. You could see the resemblance, but they also looked as mismatched as possible. Today for instance, Travis had slept in his t-shirt which was crumpled, his hair was sticking out above one of his ears and now there was a dab of strawberry on his shorts. He swiped at the berry with his thumb, which he then licked clean.

"Ewww." Tara emitted a low cry of pure sisterly disgust.

Travis smiled back at her. It was going to be a grand day, a grand day indeed.

Toggles

"Turn off that teletab Tara, you don't have any homework and we're going to be there in a minute."

Travis, Tara and their Mom were on their way to school in the Chevrolet (or Chevy as Mom jokingly called it when she was being 'old'). Tara pretended she was finishing up her homework online, but everyone knew she was chatting with her friend Xophie. Today's ride to school however included 'quality time'. Since Penelope Pruitt was still processing her morning coffee, that 'quality' was going to be exchanged between Tara and Travis.

After a few moments of scenic distraction out the window, Tara looked down at her utility belt with two toggles and silently compared it to the five toggles on Travis' bandolier. Travis knew what was bothering her. Tara was the smart one, but he had somehow managed to beat her at the Hoverpark.

"What do you have planned today?" Travis tried to open casual conversation.

"I was hoping to get at least one new toggle." Tara responded, as she looked out the window.

"That shouldn't be a problem." Travis knew his sister was brilliant in fact.

"You'd think." Tara was not as confident.

"You have to take chances Tara." Travis tried to offer a little brotherly advice. "The park rewards you for thinking out of the box."

"But it's their box." Tara argued in frustration.

"Yes, but a toggle is just a puzzle. Some puzzles are harder than others, but it's still just a puzzle. How many keys do you have?"

"I've got maybe six. But I don't know which ones I need." Tara said quietly.

"You don't have to know which ones you need. Just explore around the park and collect any keys you find. Once you have all the right keys, the portal will open. You just create whatever gadget you can with the parts available. Take the 'Hero' portal for instance, where we got this steam toy. It's like a trainer puzzle. It's the easiest to solve and it's there all the time. Collect the keys, a portal opens, you put them together and voila! Your toggle appears!"

"It's an Aeolipile." Tara said with a certain amount of frustration.

"A what?" Travis asked. Travis was a bit shocked the gadget actually had a name. Tara was not surprised.

"An Aeolipile." Tara continued, "It's considered like the first steam engine, though it really was just a toy. Hero of Alexandra invented it in the first century. So it's the first puzzle, and it's called the 'Hero' portal. I knew what keys to collect and what to make once I was in the portal."

"See? You're great at this." Travis was almost embarrassed. Tara knew much more about the history. He thought the Hero portal was called that because it was the first puzzle most people solve. As you master the puzzles, you become a 'hero' of sorts?

"I had to try the puzzle twice before I got it. Honestly Tara, I think you just need to branch out a bit and collect more keys. The keys are like a cache, a toolbox you carry with you. If you have all the parts you need for a puzzle, the portal will activate when you get close."

"You mean you don't have to figure out where to go?" Tara looked angry.

"I guess you could - I mean how would you know? Seriously, Tara, you must have done this? How did you complete that crane toggle? I don't have one of those."

It was her coolest toggle and Travis was jealous of it. He knew Tara had completed that puzzle on their last trip to the park. He had been there but he didn't always pay attention to what Tara was doing. He thought she just came upon the portal, like him.

"Well, I had all the parts, I mean it's not that hard. Once you find the block and tackle, the pulley things. I didn't know where the portal was though. A crane would be good for loading boats, but there aren't any boats on the river."

"I remember you asking about boats, but I didn't know why." Travis was truly shocked over all the effort Tara took. All that over thinking she did - was he missing something?

"Then, when we were floating around on the Gad About, I realized the crane could be used to build monuments. If you look closely at the ruins there, the block sizes change shape halfway up - from big boulders to smaller blocks. Right where they change, I noticed a difference so I went over to the ruins to investigate. The rocks started glowing and that was the portal."

"You mean you were looking for a logical place to find the portal?" Travis asked.

"Yes." Tara was a little dejected at the extra effort she obviously made.

"But that's brilliant! Tara." Travis was a bit stunned. "It's an awful lot of work though."

"Well, how do you do it?"

"I just explore. I poke around into little nooks and corners and look for the glow. Honestly, I just look for the portals."

"But how do you know what to make?"

"I don't. The portal gives me my parts. And then I just guess."

"So how did you figure out the water mill?" Tara was referring to Travis's most recent toggle. It was the most difficult one he'd done so far- there were five parts in all, which meant he had to find five keys to make it!

"I just kept trying until I got it right." Travis kept talking, ignoring Tara's angry stare. "The game master is controlling the complex puzzles. I've heard some puzzles have never been solved. The game master is making sure you're doing the work and not copying something your friend just did."

"That doesn't make any sense." Tara protested. But it did make sense to her. It was part of what made the Hoverpark so compelling. There was always something new to want, something new to do or another step to accomplish. That is how they kept people returning. At the end of the day, there would be a fresh task, a new spark to inspire guests to *Live the Wonder.* Ultimately, you could never finish the park or solve the last puzzle, so you keep coming back.

The hover technology that supported the park was developed at the University of South Florida, just after the Recovery. The University team that discovered it had originally designed several lifeboat style coastal satellites. They called them 'HoverArks' and a whole host of opportunities were pondered. One group wanted to create a series of wildlife preserves. One faction wanted to build a disaster response ship that could carry people to safety in the event of an emergency. The idea most offered in the media was a series of sustainable communities.

The design however was sold to investors for use as theme parks. They even adapted the name, changing it to Hoverpark. There was a bit of an uproar about it. The original researchers were mad, especially since a federal Innovation grant had funded the research and construction at a public university. After a strong public relations campaign which included a Florida resident discount ticket voucher most people conveniently forgot the conflict.

The Hoverpark docked at several ports along the Gulf of Mexico including Tampa. Tara and Travis went the first week it opened. The Pruitt family got complimentary tickets as part of the test market. (It was a special promotion for families who had been in the Orlando disaster.) Travis and Tara were hooked! They set aside a bit of cash every year, so they could visit when the park comes to Tampa. This year they were going with the 5th grade for the annual class fieldtrip. It worked out perfectly since the school made a special request for Penelope Pruitt, to come as chaperone.

Ms. Pruitt joining Tara's class was a bit surprising since Travis was considered the troublemaker, and probably needed more supervising. Penelope Pruitt however, figured Travis might actually do better without a 'helicopter mom.' Travis had a tendency to step up in situations of increased responsibility. Tara on the other hand could always use some extra support.

Ms. Pruitt worried more about Tara. While Tara loved the park, she was still a bit insecure and justifiably so after the Orlando disaster. Penelope Pruitt had hoped Tara would grow out of it, but over the years it seemed she just internalized things into a very cautious approach. Even as a fifth grader, Tara was attached to her mother, more so than other kids her age. So Ms. Pruitt gladly accepted the dubious honor of chaperone. She could be there with both of her kids, and she enjoyed the park as well!

By the time they pulled into the parking lot, Penelope Pruitt had finished her last cup of coffee, Travis was napping and Tara had her teletab back out and was texting Xophie (again). The Pruitt family had had enough quality time for this morning's commute. And, as Tara often argued, a little quality is sometimes enough.

3

Grayson Elementary

AT SCHOOL, THE CLASSROOM WAS literally a holding cell to contain totally jazzed kids before boarding the bus. Travis found his seat in the back, next to his best friend Hank. Hank was hard to miss, he had black curly hair, which he wore a little long to match his long lashes and big brown eyes - the perfect tools for courting favor with his teacher. Today, Hank also had a backpack filled with snacks. Hank was hungry - often. It was not a surprise, but Travis was not going to let Hank's backpack slow them down.

"You can't take all that into the park." Travis grabbed a variety pack of 'Mighty B Snacks' from Hank's pack and opened them quietly under his desk.

"What if I get hungry?" Hank protested. At the mention of hungry, almost like a reflex, Hank grabbed a pack of Mighty B Snacks himself. He hummed the song as he opened the package.

Be Strong, Be Smart, Be Powerful with Mighty Bs! The Fun Flavors with a Raucous Crunch…Mighty B Snacks pack a powerful punch!

"Look a honey bee…and a cinnamon bun, my favorite. Do you want the banana? I can't stand those."

"Nah, I'm not a fan of banana flavor either." Travis said, just as a chubby nub of a hand reached in from behind them. It was Dustin, a spike haired bully of a boy whose father worked on the Water Planning Commission. Dustin swooped down on the two of them and grabbed a bag of snacks from Hank's pack.

"Thanks for bringing enough to share" he smirked, as he ripped open the package and poured the entire contents into his mouth without looking. Travis jumped up ready to defend his friend, but Hank stopped him, shaking his head and smiling.

With the lightning speed of a gag reflex Dustin spit the snacks out into his hand…"What is this?" In horror he read the empty package out loud. "MexiMeal Worms?"

"Freak" He threw the package at them, spitting the remnants out.

Classmates were starting to gather around them; their interest peaked by the growing drama.

"What's wrong now Dustin?" Their teacher Ms. Edison was drawn to the commotion as well.

"Nothing." Dustin was wiping his tongue off on his arm, trying to clean off the chili worm flavor.

"Say it, don't spray it Dustin." Hank whispered under his breath.

"I'll get you for this." Dustin moved away to his own seat across the room.

"You helped yourself, remember?" Hank could hardly contain himself. He slid into his seat next to Travis, and grinned.

"What did you have those for anyway?" Travis was still laughing.

"Honestly, I thought it would make a good prank for Luci, being a vegetarian and all. My Aunt sent them to my Mom last year as a joke, I just sort of threw them in with everything else. I can't believe he grabbed those, of all things. How lucky is that?"

"What'd I miss?" Luci came up breathless from running and slid into her seat beside them. Her ears must have been burning, at the mention of her name. 'Luci' was short for Lucid, but very few people knew that. Appropriately, Luci was wearing a vintage 'Rhino Love' t-shirt she'd chosen just for the park. It was hip and tragic at the same time.

"Hank was sharing some snacks with the class so we can travel pack free in the park today - Just like we planned." Travis pointedly reminded him.

Hank shared the mealworm story with Luci as he reluctantly zipped up his pack and slipped it in his desk. They had agreed to take a quiet approach today - stick together, fly low under Ms. Edison's radar and have the whole day in the park to play unhindered by adult supervision. Hank and Luci were deferring to Travis, as he was definitely the park expert. Hank had been a few times, though never with Travis, and Luci had never been to Hoverpark. She'd seen the movie, because of course everyone had, but her only experience with the park proper was an excellent, though somewhat bitter, research report she wrote on the park's creation in the first 9 weeks of school. It was mostly about C.A.H.P. or Citizens against Hover Park, and how they lobbied relentlessly against the theme park.

Travis had never even heard of C.A.H.P. before Luci's report. It seemed a little overly dramatic to him. Luci thought the pressure from C.A.H.P. is what made the park so community oriented. Not only did the Hoverpark offer school discounts, they encouraged education with an emphasis on curiosity. The park combined science with thrilling rides and you could get school credit while playing the games. Hoverpark offered student grants to support alternative energy research, and it paid for school supplies for underserved kids. It was enough to convince even the most stubborn skeptics and Luci could definitely qualify as a skeptic.

Travis and Hank didn't realize that Luci's group foster home (the evil overlords as she called it) got an annual grant from Hoverpark. It was one of the reasons she knew so much about the park and its creation. She had a love/hate relationship with Hoverpark. Luci had never been able to go to the park. She hated to admit it, but she had actually been looking forward to this day for what seemed like forever. All three of them, the entire class in fact, were antsy and ready to be on their way.

Ms. Edison was attempting to review their citizenship unit, but it was obvious busywork and the students could see her irritation growing as the time kept ticking. Five minutes became ten minutes and Travis's teletab buzzed in his pocket with an illegal message from Tara in Room 32, Mrs. Van Oosten's class.

"18 bus. Only 2 in lot."

"Figures," he mumbled, sharing the message under the table with Hank and Luci as he texted back, "grrr."

"The bus probably lost a tire again on Turkey Creek Rd." Travis griped. This was so totally wrong. Not only would they lose precious time at the park, but by being late they would have to endure long lines. Travis had intended to hit the most popular ride, the Vonderheist roller coaster, first thing in the morning, just as it opened.

"You'd think they'd fix those pot holes…" Hank started, but Luci interrupted, "The road is built on a sinkhole. You can't fix a hole in the road if there's no ground to fill in on."

Luci was convinced the sinkhole situation in Florida was part of a conspiracy. In fact, Luci thought the Trans Gulf Oil Spill was also a result of sinkhole stress. She was waiting for the entire state to just collapse back into the ocean. She kept a map of all reported new sinkholes in their town on her teletab and charted the changes with the State Department maps. "See, that depression is dangerously circular in shape," she'd say. Like a crime sleuth Luci was always finding patterns, testing her theories, and otherwise wasting a brilliant mind.

"Class, I repeat, what was the name of our 43rd President's dog?"

Ms. Edison was visibly frustrated. Not only was she not up for this impromptu history review, but there were two adult chaperones in the class chatting away. Sitting on her desk and facing the class she cast a disapproving glance at the chaperones, who continued to gossip. Her mouth hardened and she returned her attention to the students. Ms. Edison was commanding in appearance, towering with broad shoulders and a pretty face even though it was half mouth. She was normally outspoken, but today she was tolerating the chaperones, tolerating the class squirming, tolerating all of it in the opportunity to enjoy the Hoverpark.

"Millie" One student shouted out.

"Not quite. Remember we are talking about George W. Bush not George Bush Sr., the 41st President." Ms. Edison pointed to a girl in the back whose hand was eternally raised in correct answers.

"Barney!"

"Right, Madison. You are correct."

Madison swished her ponytail in pride at her right answer and Ms. Edison continued, "Now can anyone tell me what kind of dog Barney was?"

Ms. Edison grew anxious as she realized her voice sounded hollow in her head. The lights were starting to glow a bit which indicated a headache might be coming on. Students began shouting out random dog types, and someone asked about Ms. Beazley. She had to control the stress! Breathe in, breath out... her eyelids closed as she practiced a deep breathing exercise. Suddenly over the intercom, there was static and the disembodied voice of the office manager.

"Attention all 5th graders, buses have arrived and we will begin boarding shortly. Please remember you represent Grayson Elementary School and remain on your best behavior for the duration of your trip."

Perky again, Ms. Edison smiled broadly, clapped her hands with invigoration and gave the students the sign to line up.

"Our chaperones, Mrs. Torez and Mrs. Nash have graciously agreed to join us today and I want you all to give them your utmost respect and courtesy."

"If I could have the chaperones join me please." She motioned to the two chatting women, "Students, I need all of you to line up by your groups. Mrs. Nash, we'll line up your group first. If you are in group one you will be with Mrs. Nash. Mrs. Torez's group, group two, will be next and if you're in group three, you're with me - you will line up last."

The class moved quickly, chairs slamming in starts and fits as students huddled to visit before organizing into a line. Hank recognized the smell of chili just before he was slapped upside the head.

"Move it dork." It was Dustin. "You're in my space. Get moving before I pummel you for breathing my air."

"Meal Worms?" Luci stepped in with a dramatic sniff. "Is that what I smell Dustin? Have you been eating meal worms again?" Luci deeply regretted missing the show this morning and was inspired to incite a little follow-up action. Dustin pushed past her roughly and moved towards Hank.

"Creep." Hank turned around and held his ground.

"What are you going to do about it loser?" Dustin rammed into Hank just as Ms. Edison waved her hand over the both of them.

"Let me make something perfectly clear," she said, "You do not have to board this bus - neither of you."

"But, he started -" Hank began with Luci and Travis nodding in agreement.

"I don't care." Ms. Edison interrupted. "I'm not refereeing you two today. Have I made myself clear?"

"Yes M'am." Hank glanced down at his right foot grinding a half circle on the floor.

"Dustin?" Ms. Edison.

"Yes, Ms. Edison." Dustin smiled like a crocodile planning his attack.

"Good. Well then, move along Dustin. You are in group one with Mrs. Nash."

Ms. Edison lifted her eyebrows at Hank, Travis and Luci.

"You're with me today. And be aware, I'm keeping my eyes on you three." She said.

The students followed Ms. Edison onto the bus. At the top of the steps, she stood at the driver's seat to insure a good view and directed the seating arrangements while the students filed past her one by one. A low beep accompanied each student as the bus monitored their biotags. Even over the din of students jabbering, Ms. Edison's voice could be heard across the bus, giving instructions.

"Absolutely not," Ms. Edison stopped Hank as he tried to join Travis in the back seat.

"Hank, you can join Sara across the aisle and Luci can sit with Travis." Hank and Travis had a knack for getting into trouble when they were together. Ms. Edison called it scheming, and considered Luci a calming influence which showed just how little Ms. Edison understood them. Luci was the one with the ideas!

As the bus pulled out of the parking lot, Ms. Edison turned around and focused on making lunch plans with the chaperones.

Travis and Hank compared toggles across the aisle. Luci had never played the park so she didn't really understand what a success Travis was at achieving the toggles.

"Do you think you can make it this time?" Hank asked.

"I'm hoping," Travis said. "I actually don't know if you get inside after you complete the seventh toggle, or if you have to collect more keys and find another portal. If I get my sixth toggle, I'm planning to head to Mt. Alta and start searching for the portal."

Hank explained it to Luci, "You need seven toggles to get access to the cave inside the park's volcano, it doesn't matter which seven. Inside the volcano is the 'cave' where the game master runs the park. If you get seven toggles, you get a private tour!"

"I read about it. They track your progress from your teletab. There's even a system to alert the game master to your progress." Luci added, "It seems pretty spooky and 'Big Brotherish' to me."

"It's a game Luci." Travis quickly chimed in. "Ms. Edison tracking us by geotag is spooky. The game master is fun. You just have to let it go and enjoy it. Start collecting keys when we get there. Some people only collect keys; you can even buy 'key' charms at the gift shop. But the real fun is in solving the puzzles. You use your keys to create gadgets. You'll love it, I promise."

"So how do you get the toggle? Or do you buy that at the gift shop too?" Luci quipped with a certain knowing look. She was not known for her patience with franchise marketing schemes.

"Toggles are free." Travis replied somewhat indignantly. "When you solve a puzzle, a nano printer in the portal creates the toggle."

"You do have to purchase the solar unit to activate it though. They sell those at the gift shops." Hank added with a certain flourish, smiling.

"One year Travis spent all his money on Marvy soda, thinking he was clever, and had to wait a whole year to activate one of his toggles."

Luci and Hank laughed as Travis swept an arm out to punch Hank in the shoulder. Ms. Edison caught the movement and eyed them with intent.

"Gentlemen?" Ms. Edison's voice of authority sliced through the bus.

"Sorry Ms. Edison." Travis and Hank replied in unison. Ms. Edison twirled her finger and Hank turned around in his seat and faced forward.

When it was safe, quietly, Travis whispered to Luci. "Yeah, it's a good idea to save a few credits for the solar unit."

4

Tampa Docks

Their bus drove slowly, crossing two sets of railroad tracks before entering the entrance ramp to I-4 into Tampa. A light fog covered the highway and what looked like steam wafted off the ponds by the ramp. As they merged, the students could see the giant cement T-Rex of the now defunct Dinosaur World. One of his arms had recently fallen off and lay alongside the entrance ramp, in a nest of shredded tire trash. All the dinosaurs were still there, in dubious condition, their paint peeling heads poking out of the palmettos and the fog. One headless velociraptor was still caught in mid leap with only a bit of rebar for a foot. He was badly in need of demolition.

All three busloads from Grayson Elementary were heading west along the interstate carefully, trying to avoid the trash and potholes. Travis peeked out the back window and waved to his

Mom sitting behind the driver in the bus behind them. The third bus was having troubles, and was still spitting puffs of black smoke as it accelerated. Eventually, the convoy settled into an easy drive at 50 mph. The interstate took them past large suburban neighborhoods, some of which were completely deserted and decaying in overgrown vegetation. By the old fair grounds was the Palm Island trailer community with its expanded pool and water park. The Seminole Casino complex loomed large over Ybor City, a beacon of lights and promises.

After a bold sweeping exit, the busses approached Tampa Docks. The normally cement and mirrored skyline gave way to hot air balloons leaning one sided on tethers and sporting heliport tour company advertisements. Some were floating above the trees, reflecting grey against the fog and smoke of an early Florida sunrise. There was a growing flurry of voices on the bus. You could hear the awe and excitement as the horizon came into view. Through the clouds and mist appeared a huge floating island. A tree covered volcano poked out of the cloud cover and the whole island hovered magically over the gulf.

The park was just as grand as the first time Travis had seen it. It floated above the horizon, like a tropical island suspended more than 2500 ft. in the air. You could see Mt. Alta, the volcano, cut with idyllic streams and lush plants, and below it, leafy 'roots' draped down a sheer face of rock and hung loose from the sky. Its size was awe inspiring.

"Oh, my," Luci whispered almost to herself, "It looks like a Fata Morgana."

"What? What is a 'Feta morgan or whatever you said?" Travis did not take his eyes off the park. It was his favorite place, he dreamed about it.

"A Fata Morgana is a fancy word for a special kind of mirage. See how it looks like there are two islands, one floating above and the other floating upside down at the dock?"

"Why would they do that?" Travis asked, perplexed. Luci was always noticing these kinds of things-it made her interesting.

"I don't know. It might just be a coincidence. It happens with boats on the horizon in Sicily. That's why the name sounds Italian. 'Fata' means 'fairy' so a Fata Morgana is supposed to be a fairy island that the witch Morgan La Fey created to draw sailors further out to sea. Morgan La Fey was the witch in King Arthur- an English story- I don't know what is up with that."

"It's pretty magical alright, but it isn't a mirage." Travis could hardly wait to get on the island.

As they arrived closer to the docks large towering solar panel trees with branches shaped like giant aerodynamic leaves rose from a parking lot. Cars were parking under the shade and some of the fancier electric ones were plugging in to the posts. The bus continued through the lot to the loading station, closer to the docks. Ms. Edison stood at the front to oversee orderly exiting, left to right, seat by seat.

Luci, Travis and Hank and stepped out into the bright Florida sun, inhaling the salt air. The adults herded the students like cattle, moving them en masse toward the park entrance. They crowded the boardwalk, crossing the bridge to the security gate, while the empty surf pounded the spotless sand below them. Load speakers played a marching band, with lots of drums and brassy horns. Over the music, an 'all knowing' female voice gave instructions in cheery, gentle tones.

"Welcome noble scientists! Boarding of the Wrenaissance Hovership has begun. Please move forward in an orderly fashion through the security gates for your bio scan. Be sure to scan your teletabs for access to the Hoverpark's digital features and photos. Follow the signs to the elevators deep inside our mother rock's root system that will carry you up to the island. At the Entrance you will find Ma Ridgley's Courtyard where you may relax from your journey skyward and purchase supplies for your adventure. Thank you for joining our efforts today. We appreciate your scientific expertise and hope you enjoy your journey."

It was inspiring, and the whole performance made the scanning and security checks seem natural. To be clear, a male voice also chimed in to add details,

"Today, we anticipate a temperature of 82 degrees with a 10 percent chance of rain. Our park hours are 8 am to 8 pm. Attractions will open at 9 am. If you have recently arrived, you are parked in Quark lot."

Travis, Hank and Luci were traveling light so they coasted through the scanners. They handed over their teletabs for scanning and walked toward the bio scanner which detected metal, chemicals and also read cortisol levels. Yes, it was an invasion of privacy as Luci reminded them all last week; but honestly, it's a private park and if you don't want to get scanned don't go to the park. Luci was beginning to grind her teeth as they waited for their turn through the scanner.

"Relax Luci, you'll set it off," Hank whispered through his teeth.

"It's all about the Orlando attacks." Travis reminded her. "They have to do it for your safety, Luci. What would you do if that happened up there?"

"I know, I know…it's still creepy though." Luci resigned to accept the scan just as they reached the equipment. All three walked through the scanners and passed, which was no surprise. There were numerous security officers at each pylon, looking over the crowd. Staffers read the scans and directed individuals through. It seemed pretty serious, thorough and exact. Travis couldn't help but be grateful for the advanced security - he had been in Orlando after all.

"Was that so hard?" Hank pressed. Luci rolled her eyes in response.

"Go to the far left, "Travis guided them to the best elevator. The line wasn't actually better, but it was his favorite view going up. From there they could see the entire gulf coast beaches below.

The 120 acre park docked to a station that rose up to meet the rock base of the park. What looked like roots winding around old gears were in fact an elaborate system of conduit, cables, cords and water pipes. Eight massive brass and glass elevators made the center 'heart' of the dock. You could face the interior if you were shy of heights, but Travis wanted a picture window view going up. He loved the look of the gulf, even though it was completely dead and had been for at least seven years. He imagined the water teaming with wildlife: fish, turtles, coral, sponges, and manatees - it must have been incredible.

That was before the Trans Gulf Oil Spill, the disaster that killed everything - in the water and on the ocean bed. Every year, some kid finds a coral or a coquina shell on the beach and the media pounces on what it calls, "encouraging signs of recovery," but no one is fooled. The gulf is not healing; it's just festering out there. Some old timers say what we need is a storm like no other, a huge cleaning hurricane - but most everyone else has given up hope.

Their elevator car was full. One small child clutching a pair of sun goggles held his Mom's hand in the back of the car. Luci offered to let him in front of her, but his Mom shook her head emphatically and mouthed 'thank you.' The view going up wasn't for everyone. The elevators began rising with the sound of trumpets, the soundtrack for their ride up was a full orchestra.

As they slowly lifted up over the crowd, Travis searched for his Mom and Tara. It was fun watching people below drift away like ants. He found his Mom by her cowboy hat at the bag security check emptying her backpack while Tara walked through the scanner. Luci gently jabbed him with her elbow and laughed.

"What is up with that guy?" She pointed to an overdressed fellow with blond dread locks and a cane in line just behind Tara. He was wearing a crazy looking tattered bowler hat and a heavy coat which was too warm for Florida.

"Someone needs to call the fashion police - let them know the 90s have escaped!" Hank was a people watcher too.

Just as the crazy looking man approached the scanner, a woman beside him reached over and attacked Tara who recoiled in alarm! From the elevator, it looked like the woman was screaming, grabbing at Tara's hair as alarms went off and flashing red lights alerted security. The elevator stopped rising and paused, giving them a bird's eye view of the drama unfolding below them. They watched Travis's Mom run toward Tara, only to be held back by security. Travis could see her arguing with one of the gate guards.

"They won't let her pass!" Travis said helplessly. Why wouldn't they let his Mom go over to Tara? Travis knew Tara was naturally nervous…well, maybe it was a learned nervous…but nervous in any case. She really needed their Mom. Beside him Hank was looking around and behind, growing increasingly alarmed.

"The elevator has stopped moving." Hank was obviously not pleased with that development. "Why isn't the elevator moving?" He stared at the ceiling, willing the elevator to start climbing.

"Don't do it Hank." Luci gave him a warning look, glancing back at the kid with his Mom. Hank understood and closed his eyes, silently willing the elevator to move, to just start.

Down below all movement stopped as a small crowd gathered in front of the elevators. Travis stood watching closely. Tara and his Mom stood out clearly as the only people by the scanners not in a security uniform. The red lights stopped. Over to the side, the woman who caused the ruckus was lying on the ground, her hands cuffed behind her back. She was hysterical, writhing and obviously carrying something metal, which security confiscated. Travis couldn't tell what it was but he noticed the guards had let his Mom pass. Tara was clinging to her Mom, and nodding her head.

Gently, the elevator began moving again, much to Hank's relief and guests began entering the scanner turnstiles again. As the elevator rose, Travis watched security officers escorting the woman away and with a sigh of relief he saw Tara and his Mom approach the elevators.

"Did you see that!!!" Luci said again.

"Yeah - very scary! I can't believe that woman chose Tara, of all the people down there!" Travis was still anxious.

"Did you see what she had?" Hank asked, anxious in a different way.

"No, it didn't look like a weapon. They stopped her though, and I saw Mom and Tara move on to the elevator, so its fine."

Travis was greatly relieved to see Tara with his Mom. Hank nodded, distracted, but Luci was not so easily calmed.

"No. It's not fine." Luci contradicted him. "I was watching that strange guy Travis. He went through the gate at the same time as Tara. And, I'm pretty sure the alarm went off *before* the crazy woman ran through the scanner."

"I don't know, it looked like that woman set off the alarm."

"I don't think so Travis. That man ran through the scanner and disappeared right after he went through the gate."

"You might have lost him in all the chaos." Travis was not going to let this day be ruined.

"But I can't even find him in the crowd."

"What are you talking about?" Hank was sometimes impatient with Luci's conspiracies and he didn't want the question answered. He didn't really follow all of Luci's ideas, and honestly he often considered her nervous questions general 'static.' He moved his attention to the gulf, dismissing Luci's concerns.

"I'm sure it's OK." Travis said without conviction.

Luci didn't respond. Her jaw set, she scanned the crowd; looking for a hint of that bowler hat. Travis instead focused on the empty surf below and tried to think about the day ahead of them. Luci was always one for pointing out the negative. Unfortunately, it was Travis's experience that she was rarely wrong.

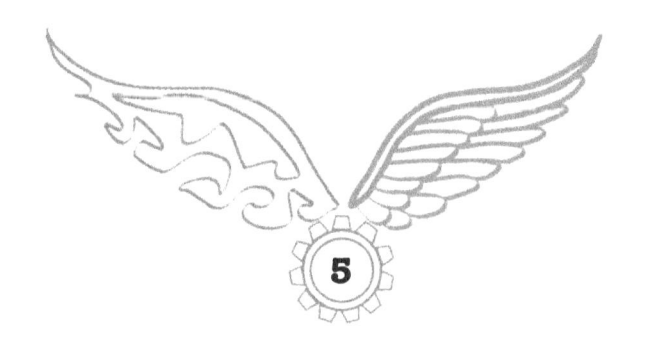

Welcome

THE ELEVATOR CONTINUED ITS ASCENT, slowly moving up to the park accompanied by the Hoverpark's audio welcome story. The story effects were so realistic it scared some of the more timid park visitors and the soundtrack had to be toned down the first year. It still began appropriately, with a brass band fanfare. The songs welcomed the parkers with trumpets, trombones and drums and served as an introduction for 'Dr. Wren' and his colleagues. Not surprisingly, the audio character of Dr. Wren spoke in a strong British accent. It was a voice that inspired images of a Victorian mustached gentleman.

"*Welcome to the MEEAD Research Center for Mechanical Engineering, Energy and Alternative Design. I am Dr. Chuck Wren, Principal and Lead Investigator of Hover Technology. I am joined today by my prestigious colleagues, Drs. Amy Aime and Frederick*

Vonderheist. Please accept our sincere thank you for your interest in our work here at the MEEAD Center. We began our scientific inquiry into alternative energy sources but quickly developed major achievements in Hover technology. Our work here is highly acclaimed by the scientific community and we anticipate a cadre of high rolling investors and scientists like yourselves to join in our efforts. We have prepared a rather humble gala in the ballroom to showcase our accomplishments and celebrate the new 'Wrenaissance' if you will! Ha, ha..."

(Dr. Wren's voice was suddenly drowned out by sounds of chaos. There are outbursts of people tussling and whispering. Doors open and close revealing loud explosions and alarms in the background.)

"Pardon me Dr. Wren." *A new voice, one with a German accent, addressed Dr. Wren.*

"We have got a problem. A fissure has opened in the crust of the earth. I don't know how that happened. There is a cone rising - obviously a volcano. What do you want me to do?"

"Excuse me a moment Fredrick..." *Dr. Wren mumbles and then addresses the visitors in the elevator again.*

"Forgive me folks; we've got a busy lab you know! My services are required in the Hoverlab. Amy, please take over for me."

"But..."

"Please address our GUESTS Amy."

There is the sound of steps leaving, then silence, and a hesitant tapping on the microphone.

"Yes, an…unexplained geo-thermal accident-I mean **incident**-has recently…umm… interrupted experiments in the HoverLab. As a result of several unforeseen… complications… we must delay our-Yes, well-we express our sincere regrets at this unexpected turn of events, and apologize for any inconvenience this may have caused."

There are loud confident steps again, heralding the return of Dr. Wren who interrupts Amy.

"Nonsense Amy, the show must go on! Pardon our dust, as they say! We've got nothing to hide. An impromptu - ah, er - demonstration of our recent accomplishments in Hover Technology has resulted in a phenomenal example of the potential for alternative energy! Drs. Aime, Vonderheist and I are somewhat indisposed at the moment, but we will open our labs at 9:00 am. In the meantime, I invite you to explore the MEAD Center Island, yes I said island! Our staff, Sami and Sue Namee, is at your disposal and offer guest services and information. Ma Ridgely at the cafeteria has prepared a sumptuous feast in anticipation of your arrival. Thank you again for joining us today. Enjoy!"

As the elevator enters into the enclosed shaft of the park platform transporting them to the surface, the elevator lights came on. The scientists are overheard talking among themselves.

"Incredible! It's absolutely incredible - Did you see that?"

"Sir, I think it's active. There's been some destruction in the labs; almost certainly a lack of stabilization." Dr. Amy Aime warns Dr. Wren.

"*Nonsense, it's beautiful! Where is Dr. Vonderheist? Frederick?*" You could hear the sound of exiting footsteps followed by a last direct plea from Dr. Amy Aime as she addresses the elevator again.

"*Please, we have lost several critical keys to our experiments and we need your help to find them. If you see something glowing, use your teletab to collect it. If you're feeling lucky, I've opened several portals throughout the island where we can try to piece together some of the gadgets. Thank you in advance. Good luck and stay inspired!*"

The last statement was timed perfectly to the opening of the elevator doors and the guest's first view of Hoverpark. The effect was quite dramatic. The bright sun of the open sky glistened off steam emitting from the volcano, Mt. Alta. It practically glowed above the bustling tropical village of Ma Ridgely's courtyard. Behind a grand fountain centerpiece was the main gateway. A bold metal logo was created out of rivets and cogs and held up by ancient stone columns. Small clouds shaded the park from the sun and a light mist rose from the ponds and fountains hidden among the trees and shrubs.

They walked along with other Parker traffic moving towards a patio of lush gardens, guest services kiosks and Ma Ridgely's Cafeteria. There were restrooms, information kiosks where you scan your teletab and gift shops. If you didn't want to wait in line at the cafeteria, tables were connected to a limited menu instaserve system from which you could order basics like coffee, juice, fruit, donuts, bagels, breakfast salad and extra condiments.

Mesmerized, Hank started to move over to one of the tables but Ms. Edison was quickly behind him.

"No Sir," She said. "We're meeting in the Group Tours Bay."

She escorted them across the entrance to the Group Tours Bay, where large groups gathered. Each group was assigned a bay where special education features of the park were coordinated in advance and waiting for them. Ms. Edison was gathering their class with the rest of their school at the student benches in Shell Bay.

A smiling Hoverpark educator greeted Ms. Edison and confirmed their curriculum. Over the din of excited students, Ms. Edison was shouting, "Class, I'd like you to begin your adventure here at the 'Science in Motion' boards. You will find instructions and helpful tips on collecting and tagging artifacts in your field journals for class credit."

Classmates poked reluctantly at the boards designed to 'edutain' school groups while they waited. The programs appealed to teachers, but the class found them infinitely boring. Everyone that is, except Sandy Higgens, who loved boring lists and avidly read her great-great grandparent's encyclopedia.

"Over here…" Travis was dragging Hank and Luci over to a board that was far away from Ms. Edison and the chaperones.

Luci and Hank were not easily persuaded to follow Ms. Edison's instructions. It wasn't like Travis to just comply. They all hated digital learning, particularly the kind that schools tried to shove down their throats.

"Seriously, Travis?" Luci was especially surprised, but joined him reluctantly at one of the boards. Hank held back, looking around, nervous that someone else might notice them actually at the boards. Hank didn't want to risk being seen learning.

"Come on Travis, someone's going to see us." Hank complained.

"Patience Grasshopper" Travis grinned as he activated the screens. He wasn't at the board to get Ms. Edison's instructions. He had a plan. He backed out of the education programs and began searching for the park's interactive coaster designer. Travis knew coaster design was part of a middle school physics curriculum offered at the park, so the program had to be accessible from the board. It was fantastic-you could prepare a coaster and then ride it later in the day on a simulator in the park!

"It has to be here?" Travis flipped through the menu finally locating the 'Design a Coaster' application.

"Voila" He turned to smile broadly at his friends with a flourish of his hand over the screen. Dramatically, a schematic coaster rose up from the board in brilliant 3-D. Suddenly interested, Hank stepped up beside Travis and pushed on the track tentatively - it moved! Everything could be manipulated directly. At his side, Travis started adding options on the track.

"Are you sure you have time?" Luci was drawn to the coaster watching intently.

"You doubt me?" Travis laughed, "This is one I started last spring. I am finishing it to-day."

"Go on- try it. See the red? That's the g-force indicator; it means the coaster isn't safe. I'm making the loop a little more tear shaped so there's enough speed to get through it. It's that whole kinetic energy thing, you're using motion and gravity to help drive the car through the loop."

There was a curve mid way that still had a lot of red. It was a pretty simple fix Travis thought, and he wanted to give Hank and Luci a chance to build.

"You guys can help adjust that curve by moving those pylons up and down a little until the red is gone. I'm adding some scenic 4D."

Travis added a water pool at the base of one of the drops, and he activated 'splash' and 'wind' elements as well as 'chasing comets' in the barrel roll and 'heat' in the first rise which was dark. Travis had also added music, but he didn't want to tell Hank what it was so he did it on the sly.

With all of them bent over the 'Science in Motion' boards making changes to the coaster, Hank stole a vigilant glance up at the park, to see if anyone else had noticed them. He spied One-Eyed Cy, the Security Chief, coming around the corner with his service dog. Officer Cyrus Pinter was a legend on and off Hoverpark. Most everyone was terrified of him, his appearance alone was shocking, and Cy didn't do much to soften the edges.

Half of his face was burned as a result of some horrible accident. He had a scar running across his forehead and over his eye, but the most alarming feature was an old eye patch, straight out of the 20th century. While he had a park uniform on, and standard issue shoes, he was definitely on the fringe as far as friendly customer service at the park was concerned.

Cy was a firm believer in fear tactics. He was well aware that his ominous appearance served as a deterrent for pranksters, and he emphasized it with regular scowls and glowering looks. Cy didn't like kids. In fact, he barely liked adults, and he had a strong aversion to any guests going off the beaten path. In the mornings, Cy liked to gloom about at the entrance as a discouraging influence to any ne'er-do-wells. He paid particular attention to school groups, and liked to stomp around in view of the tour bays.

"It's One - Eyed Cy" Travis stared quietly.

"That's not nice." Luci reprimanded him. "Even if he is mean." She mumbled quietly. Luci was familiar with the stories about Cy, and she stole a quick look at the man behind the legend.

"Jeepers! I'd swear his patch has grown even bigger and patchier!" Hank was easily intimidated by scary adults. "I don't know why they have him around. I can't imagine anyone actually approaching him for help."

"Oh crap - I almost forgot!" Travis exclaimed, suddenly pulling his teletab out of a pocket on his utility belt and holding it over the park logo in the home menu. It blinked for a quick moment and then a Hoverpark logo glowed on the screen. "We need to sign in if we're going to play the park. Ms. Edison is absolutely right about that. If we do it here, we'll avoid the lines."

Hank pulled his tethered teletab out from his belt and held it over the screen, but Luci suddenly began looking around the benches frantically. "Oh, no - guys, I think I lost my purse - my teletab is in my purse."

Hank sighed. Girls and their purses. "You need to get a Hoverpark belt Luci. Or a cuff or something."

"You can ask One - eyed Cy if he found it" Travis quipped.

"Shut up Travis. This is serious." Luci was beginning to panic. She couldn't afford to lose her teletab. Luci's situation was a bit different than Travis or Hank. She lived in a government sponsored foster home. Her teletab was not an accessory; it was almost all she owned.

"No reason to freak out, it will show up. It's not like anyone else can use it Luci..." Travis knew how fragile Luci's world could get. Honestly, he was convinced it would show up.

"It would really suck if you didn't have one today." Hank's voice chimed in and trailed off as he realized his mistake. He was not always the best at comforting girls.

"Think Luci," Travis looked up from the coaster, "Did you leave it on the bus?"

"No, no, I had it checked at security remember?" Luci was quiet. Without her teletab, she'd have to rent one for the day to complete her assignment. Calm, Calm - "I must have left it on the elevator."

"That's good." Travis reassured her, "It will be in lost and found then. It's over there next to guest services - You'll have to get Ms. Edison or one of the other chaperones to take you."

Hank smiled at that. He'd been a little worried they would have to go with her. He knew Travis was a gentleman and while he didn't mind helping, there were coaster pylons to adjust! They watched as Luci crossed the bay to where Ms. Edison was sharing the schedule with the chaperones. He could see Mrs. Nash reluctantly volunteer to walk her over to guest services - Poor Luci. Mrs. Nash was an authoritative Mom who constantly referred to her 'Sullen Teen Handbook' on her teletab. Her daughter Sydney was in their class but Travis hardly knew her. She was what people call 'quiet.' Travis was sure it would be fine though, and he couldn't miss this opportunity to finish his coaster.

The last of their classmates were leaving the elevators and Travis was growing anxious. They were still waiting for his Mom and Tara to arrive, but everyone else was there. He summoned his most nonchalant voice and asked "Hank, how are we doing on the G-Force?"

"Almost done, but I can't fix this?" Travis stepped up to see what Hank was talking about. Flashing red bars kept streaming over the track just at the third curve, where the coaster came out of a barrel roll. The spot was tricky because the curve needed to be banked, and Hank was trying to move the height of both pylons. Ok. He had this. Travis scrolled over and modified a few of the exterior pylons and voila! The coaster began running smoothly and an AR e-ticket appeared good for 6 guests at 2:00pm.

"Yes!" Travis smiled and Hank celebrated with a little dance move he called the Hankster Hula! While Travis was downloading the ticket, a glittering spiral suddenly splashed across the screen and spun into a glowing ornate shaped key.

"Whoa!" Hank exclaimed in awe. "You got another one!"

Elated, Travis quickly scanned the key with his teletab only to hesitate slightly when he read what the key was - "It's a hack key? That's weird. It wasn't for completing the coaster; it was for bypassing the education software!"

"What?" Hank leaned in to see the key, but there was no time to pause and wonder. Mrs. Pruitt and Tara had finally arrived at the Bay.

A loud buzz of students and activity welcomed Travis's Mom and Tara. They were surrounded by Ms. Edison, the other chaperones and a group of the students who had seen the spectacle. Travis moved easily through the crowd to the front. Mrs. Pruitt didn't normally like so much attention, but the adrenaline was coursing through her and Tara was still a bit shaken, so she stepped up as storyteller.

"We were in line for the scanners - I was a bit behind Tara because I had gone through bag check first. I couldn't believe it when the whole ruckus started."

Tara was quiet, choosing instead to seek out Xophie, who had arrived reluctantly on a different elevator and now pushed through the crowd to stand beside her. Mrs. Pruitt elaborated on the story for her.

"That crazy woman grabbed at Tara and set off the alarms. I can't imagine what was going through her head. She was carrying a pair of root clippers! What on earth would she do with those up here?"

"Don't you mean 'what on Hoverpark' Mrs. Pruitt? You said 'what on earth'." Xophie was a bit of a quibbler. "Hoverpark isn't on earth."

"That's funny Xophie…." Mrs. Pruitt paused patiently before continuing, "And the cops - I mean security guards - wouldn't let me through. I kept telling them Tara was my daughter but they wouldn't let me pass until Tara confirmed it. I think they checked her bio account?"

Tara nodded in silent confirmation. At the edge of the group, Luci was back with Mrs. Nasta. She clutched her purse and listened intently to the story.

"Did they mention if she was alone Mrs. Pruitt?" Luci tried to shout over the other students. She had to yell even louder to get through.

"Was she working alone Mrs. Pruitt?" Luci shouted.

"What do you mean, Luci? I assure you, she was very much alone. Give or take a pair of root clippers."

"I hope they gave you a pass or something." The group had started to lose focus. "Did you get a photo? I tried but it wouldn't take through the glass."

"No, but thanks...." Penelope Pruitt was trying to accommodate everyone's best intentions, but she was done speculating. "OK, let's not squander our time- we're all here safe and sound and there's a fruitatta with my name on it at La Ceiba!"

Luci, however, wasn't ready to let go quite yet, "It still seems strange to me. Why go through all that drama just to bring root clippers into the park?" She asked no one in particular.

6

On Maps

"ALRIGHT STUDENTS, IF I CAN have everyone's attention - over here please Dustin - the faster we do this, the faster you will get into the park. Let's line up quickly in our groups. Your chaperone will distribute a geotag and you will receive one pass. Let's go students."

Travis, Hank and Luci assembled at the back of Group 1 around Ms. Edison who was synching teletabs to create temporary geotags for the group. The geotags were one of the best parts of the park. Adults could track you, but you were free from 'satellite' chaperones. Better still, every synched teletab received a complimentary E-pass to cut line in one attraction. So, Ms. Edison would know where they were, and their proximity to 'hotspots' identified by park security as inappropriate places for students. In exchange, they got to wander the park freely and enjoy their pass at any ride of their choice.

If you cleared your geotag, not only did it cost you your pass, but you were condemned to being nanny'd for the remainder of the trip. The pass was an icon shaped like a flame (or the back end of a diving duck) that remained on the map in your teletab until you used it. All the school groups got them as part of their tour package.

"Travis, Hank and Luci - I need you over here please." Ms. Edison was not going to let them ruminate long on the early morning drama. "You are with me today. I will be the one following your geotags."

Travis, Luci and Hank synched their teletabs. Travis couldn't wait to get into the park. Hank was practically jumping with excitement. They couldn't help but notice though, that while Luci had her purse and teletab, her face was screwed up in worry.

"What's wrong?" Travis whispered as they waited for the rest of their classmates to get their geotags. He hated to admit it but he didn't really want to know.

"Remember that strange man with the coat and hat?" She said. "Well, the coat, hat and a dreadlock wig were being processed in lost and found when we got there. That's bad Travis." Luci glanced around the crowd as she emphasized her concern. "Really, really bad."

Why did she always have to find something to worry about? Travis was silent, trying to think of something pleasant to say and was relieved by Ms. Edison as she interrupted the students chatter.

"Groups 1, 2 and 3 - I need everyone in my class over here please" Ms. Edison addressed the students who huddled excitedly, waiting to be set free to explore the park.

"You are representing your school and your class today. I know that you will behave yourselves accordingly while in the park. You have an assignment today. I've activated several themes we've been following in class, and these are synched to our teletabs. The themes are energy and natural science. Your assignment is to collect or tag objects related to these themes in your field notebook. Once collected, you can scroll through the curator details on your tagged item and create a label for your personal gallery. You must collect and label at least seven items to receive a grade and homework pass for today."

"Last but not least," Ms. Edison looked long and hard at the class. "I want to remind you that the geotags are a privilege. If you abuse this privilege, I will personally escort you for the remainder of the day. Do not ruin my trip to the park by making me staff an in park detention. Are we clear?"

Wholeheartedly, the class echoed "Yes, Ms. Edison."

"Then you have fun today! We will meet at 8:00 pm at the Shell Bay exit. You will exit the park at Shell Dock, across the plaza from the Centrifuge. Follow the color white to Shell Bay where our buses will meet us. Do not be late. OK?"

"Yes Ms. Edison." The class was getting antsy now. Travis scanned the bay, quickly finding his Mom, who smiled back at him from across the benches and pointed to her teletab. As chaperone for Tara's class, she was monitoring eight students, including geotags for Tara and her friends Xophie and Monica. Travis knew his Mom would be riding the GENSys with them, it was their favorite ride. He also knew if he needed her she was just a 'tell' away.

"OK, what's our plan?" Travis, Luci and Hank were huddled together at the fountain to coordinate their maps and plan their day at the park.

"Obviously we need to get to the Vonderheist early." Travis reminded them. We have tickets for 2:00 p.m. at the Wrenaissance Theatre of Wonders- that's our coaster. What else do you guys want to do?"

The Hoverpark map depicted the M.E.E.A.D. Research Center showing the Mt. Alta volcano rising through the hover lab and other research labs in varying forms of disarray. The sail train along the perimeter was still intact but Dr. Wren's Hoverlab lay in shambles beside the Centrifuge Hot Air Balloon. There was Dr. Vonderheist's air ship hanger where the roller coaster track wound around a crumbling wind farm. The GENsys, a 4D film planetarium experience on the south side of the island was still in perfect condition, though several ruins in the plaza seemed to be suffering. A cracked hydroelectric dam formed the edge of Sue Namee's wave pool and a docking area for the Gad About lazy river.

"Definitely the Vonderheist…I also want to ride the GENSys." Luci checked off each attraction as they listed it.

"I vote we ride The Fracker at least once? It's a blast." Hank loved the Fracker. He wasn't real sure of the GENSys or the Vonderheist but he loved the Fracker.

"Is that the water flume? Will we get wet?"

"Yes. Yes it is and yes, you will!" Travis loved the Fracker as well and he wanted to get as close to the volcano as possible - just in case.

"And the Centrifuge…" Luci checked off the spinning air balloon.

"Yes the Centrifuge, but the Vonderheist is our first stop - we need to get there early before the line builds." Travis had a plan. Besides, Luci loved an adrenaline rush and Hank was usually easy to convince. He might hesitate at first, but the fear of ridicule always won him over.

"Which way is the fastest?" Luci asked.

"Left" Travis answered. "We should go left. Most people naturally go to the right. There will be less traffic this way."

By 'left,' Travis meant going through Bee Plaza on the left of Ma Ridgely's Courtyard, which was packed with families milling about. Travis, Hank and Luci passed adults enjoying coffee and ice cream served in the fruit husk. They avoided groups of kids playing in water spouts around the gardens. Families were huddled together, looking over their teletabs, checking bio accounts and organizing their trips. Groups of serious parkers were easy to pick out; in high fashion they wore toggles on utility belts or attached to hats.

The fastest way took them past the Hoverpark science supply store. The shop was under a sign with a large bee and it had small honeycombed cabinets and nooks where you could find utility belts, gadget jewelry, goggles, hats, sunscreen, and t-shirts. They avoided the key charm center. They were trying to cut through quietly but as Luci passed the plushy 'Rescue Center', one of the little stuffed monkeys reached out to her and said 'Mama Lucid'.

"Whoa!!" Hank exclaimed. That one's yours Luci!

Luci gently picked up the plush monkey and examined the little creature curiously. He was cute, and very soft, his big eyes seemed to be moving. "Mama Lucid," said the monkey a second time.

"It's a digital recognition program," She said, scanning him with her teletab for the price - $52! With a tiny huff of disgust she returned it to the shelf. "They must upload your scanned info into the store here so the plushies will 'recognize' you."

"Hyper impulse marketing" Travis laughed. "That same monkey will recognize another 'Mama' in like five minutes."

"It's pretty creepy if you ask me." Luci predictably dismissed the ploy.

Hank looked at her and grinned. "It almost worked. You would have bought it if it was reasonably priced."

They walked along the river's edge, to the right of the sun dial. Across the plaza was the GENsys glowing in the sun like the Taj Mahal. It was a domed monument shining in a reflection pool. Two gently sloping walkways on either side of the pool led inside, which was adorned in elaborate tiles. Luci stopped in awe for a moment- the GENsys was probably the most popular ride on the park. Inside the theatre, guests were lifted in their seats up and out into the galaxy, exploring the birth of stars, novas, sweeping past a black hole and experiencing a solar flare. The theatre was an interactive Imax, that moved like a planetarium projector. The high definition imagery was stunning, 60 frames a second.

"Luci, come on!" Travis called.

Luci had stopped again to admire the leaf material of one of the large trees. "It's a solar cell!" She said almost to herself.

"Sure" Travis nodded. "Almost half the plants on Mt. Alta are solar units powering the park." He could see the lights going on in Luci's mind. She looked up with wonder at the volcano. "You didn't know that?" Travis was surprised. Luci was usually an expert on eco-friendly technology.

"I knew they used solar cells, but I didn't know they'd look so real! I guess I thought the park's energy systems would look more industrial."

"Sometimes they do, but not in Bee Plaza."

"So, everything is themed, even the utilities?"

"I guess, I never really thought about it. Now that you mention it, we could probably tag this plant for our gallery."

"Already done," interrupted Luci, smiling. "Weren't we headed somewhere?"

Travis, Luci and Hank walked along a path past yellow tulip trees in full glorious bloom. The path led to Amy's Conservatory. A large Ceiba tree had fallen across the river creating a natural bridge of sorts to Mt. Alta, though a fence prevented guests from using it. Travis was moving 'as the crow flies' and ducked into the Dr. Amy Aime's bioenergy research lab. From inside, they could see the roots of a roof garden growing through the ceiling. It looked like the irrigation system was part of the condensation from the air conditioning. It was ingenious, and Luci wondered if that was happening all over the island.

A working bio generator, powered by potatoes, grew against the back wall masking a service entrance. The generator actually ran a mister and the lighting for the lab. Several employees in coveralls with the MEEAD Center logo were pushing carts into a mundane door labeled 'lab technicians only.' A desk, obviously

Dr. Amy Aime's, had a dog water dish and a little dog bed beside it for her Scottish terrier, Mona.

Hank peeked into an adjoining room and saw several tables covered with the bones of animals, laid out like a puzzle. Hanging from the ceiling, by a workbench covered in wires and bones, was the skeletal remains of a mammoth grouper fish in mid chomp. He actually ducked a bit to avoid the grouper which clinked in anticipation above him. A hand painted sign above a desk said, 'The Bone Room.' The whole building was glowing red on their teletab maps, which meant they could complete their assignment here-something to keep in mind for later.

"Wow." Luci was stopped in front of a stunning mosaic of miniature tiles on the wall, labeled "The Art of Progress."

"Wow indeed." Hank stood beside her, admiring the artwork. It depicted the river Euphrates which branched out into the Fertile Crescent to roll into Mesopotamia. The river trickles across to ancient Egypt through blooming fireworks in Asia, and further into Greco-Roman Temples and aqua ducts. The architecture and tall ships of Europe reached upward and one side of the stream ran into the Americas, from Chichen Itza to Tortuga, to Cony Island's Ferris wheel. Various ships were traveling along the harbors through rising mountains, greeted by trees and animals. The Ferris wheel actually became a water wheel of sorts flowing across to create an ocean horizon from which rose a stylized ship, unmistakably the Hoverpark.

Luci reached up to touch the mural and was surprised to find her hand was wet. It could just be dew, but it seemed like the water was really flowing! She scanned across the mural with her teletab and various windows of information bubbled up as she paused over the pictures. A note on the legend of the hanging gardens in Mesopotamia gave way to a history of the Ferris wheel. She could spend an hour here just reading about inventions and world history.

"Come on, Luci." the insistent sound of Travis' voice trailed off as he moved through the doors. Hank kept pace behind him. At the sound of the door closing, Luci jumped up and ran after them. Travis and Hank were loping along a side path of the plaza. Luci quickly caught up.

"Did you know you can read information about all the things here on the park, the pictures and the artifacts?" Luci was absolutely stunned by the possibilities.

"Yeah, they have lots of stuff like that on Hoverpark. It's all connected." Travis dismissed the technology. He was only interested in the rides and the game. And right now, he was in a hurry to get to the Vonderheist before the rest of the guests.

"Let's take this side path." Travis ducked to the right through a stand of trees and Luci and Hank cornered quickly to follow him.

"What about the sail train?" Hank disrupted their progress with a good question. Just past the Conservatory, the train was still in the station. Luci paused to watch its sails luff in the breeze, a white fluttering over crowds of boarding families.

"We can walk faster." Travis replied. "And I mean walk faster - come on guys! There'll be plenty of time to gawk this afternoon. We'll come back, I promise."

7

The Vonderheist

They reached the Vonderheist promptly at 9:00, narrowly beating the 'Vonderheist Parade' of parkers following a staffer wearing pilot pants, flight cap and scarf, marching with pomp and a megaphone, calling for 'Volunteers in Flight'. Travis, Luci and Hank managed to maneuver into the gate just before they arrived and they watched smiling as the crowd filed into line winding around the wind turbines in the wind farm. It was particularly satisfying to watch Dustin and two of his friends arguing in line.

The Vonderheist was not for the timid. An incredible coaster, it rose like a giant machine of rusted bolts and rivets, cogs and wheels; a great looping contraption that dropped through unknown cement towers, and swept through wind turbines along the rim of the park. The cars looked like various ancient aircraft experiments from da Vinci to the Wright Brothers and each plane was named: Borelli, Hooke, Frost and Cayley to mention just a few. The track swept up and out over the edge of the park offering unbelievable views of both the park and the shoreline below.

Travis, Hank and Luci followed the line of increasingly excited guests as they approached the entrance which wove through the air craft hanger of Dr. Vonderheist. A young boy was shunted from the line with an irate adult when he didn't meet the height restrictions at the door. As they entered the building, a booming voice like a drum through the music repeated a strong warning in numerous languages:

"Due to the nature of the research center, please be aware that this attraction may be extraordinarily frightening to certain individuals. Drops of 80 feet along the edge of the island appear to be drops of 2700 ft back to the earth's surface. A mandatory bioscan is required to confirm your suitability for this attraction. Guests with heart conditions, high blood pressure or a history of anxiety are not permitted to ride. If you are pregnant you will not be permitted to ride. If you have never ridden a roller coaster, do not attempt this ride. If you are not completely thrilled with the idea of heights and prefer to have your feet on the ground, do not attempt this ride. If you are wondering whether or not you should try this attraction… you are strongly advised not to board the Vonderheist."

Laughing they moved inside the hanger, the warnings trailed off and they followed the line through an abandoned office where bright red lights flashed across numerous computer screens and reflected in a large black and white photo poster of Chicago's Wrigley Field. A hand copter lay by an old coffee cup and in the corner of the ceiling, wrapped in cobwebs; a doll was tied to a kite. The line proceeded through a mud room past lab coats and leather flight helmets hung from coat hooks along the wall. One red scarf hung by a pair of dusty goggles. Handwritten notes were tacked on the wall.

A sketch tacked above the flight goggles detailed a riveted joint imitating an articulated wing. Teletab in hand, Luci paused over the sketch to see more information on the wing. It was a Da Vinci design for an Ornithopter, a glider - she recognized the picture. Just as Luci started walking past it, the jointed wing began to glow and with a press of a button, she quickly snagged the key.

"Fantabulous!" She smiled admiring the image on her teletab.

"You got your first key Luci!" Travis said as Hank quickly reached over with his teletab and tried to capture the same key. A quick info tab on DaVinci's flying machines popped up, with some historic diary entries but the wing wouldn't glow.

"You know each key only works once a day." Travis laughed. "But you keep trying Hank."

"It was worth a try," Hank shrugged. And then after an uncomfortable pause in the silent stare of his friend he added sheepishly, "Good job Luci."

"So, what do I do with a wing?" Luci wasn't sure she understood the whole gadget creation game.

"You could be making a flying machine, or maybe all you really need is the idea of a wing? Sometimes you just don't know what you need until you get there." Travis added.

"Sometimes we don't even know we're there." Hank couldn't help himself. Luci tolerated the two of them, pleased with her funky looking wing. In good spirits, they trailed along in the line slowly as it wound into the main hanger.

Inside were flying machines and airplane prototypes in various stages of repair. Lots of the tool boxes were open and a loud alarm echoed through the hollow room. As they moved closer to the open dock at the end of the hanger, you could see blue space only, with the occasional cloud. It gave the appearance they would be flying off the edge of the park.

Hank's eyes visibly doubled in size as they moved closer to the dock. To their right, a large sign half- painted read, "Vonderheist Travel: We put the 'Get' in Getting There!"

While there was the impression of a lot of work going on in the shop, the hanger seemed quickly abandoned, with the exception of the boarding crew and the guests. Wrenches were laid haphazardly across benches, work belts were hanging from scaffolding; and one tool box had obviously been knocked over, its contents spilling out on the floor.

"Please step forward into the bioscan," a young lady gestured to the docking queue. Travis and Luci went through the scan fine, but just as Hank moved in, the yellow warning lights went off and he was pulled to the side. Travis and Luci stepped out of queue with Hank as an employee named 'Bob' attempted to explain the situation.

"I'm sorry," Bob said, "But the scanner has indicated you might not be safe on this ride. I'm not sure what caused this, but I can't allow you to board." Hank starred at his feet in embarrassment as Bob continued," I am truly sorry for any inconvenience this may have caused. I assure you, it is for your own safety."

"What's happening, Hank?" Travis and Luci gathered round.

"It says I can't ride." Hank responded with more than a hint of indignation. It was one thing to be afraid of a ride, but quite another to be told he couldn't ride it!

"Could be a mistake - it's probably a mistake - is there anything in your medical history?" Luci talked as she thought. "Do you have asthma? Or a heart murmur?"

"Are you pregnant?" Travis couldn't help himself. Luci punched him in the arm.

Hank glared at Travis and turned back to the employee named 'Bob' who continued, "The scanner doesn't tell us why, it's a privacy issue." Bob paused to look pointedly at Travis. "If you feel the scanner made an error, you can go to Guest Services and they may be able to assist you. I'm sorry but I can only accept overrides from guest services. I can offer you a snack credit - good for one slice, a snack pack or a Marvy soda, to compensate for your time in line?"

"Thanks. I'll take it!" Hank visibly cheered up as Bob swiped his teletab with the park wand.

"You two go on without me." Hank waved Travis and Luci back into the line. "Hup two folks, always take your turn when you have one."

Travis and Luci hesitated.

"Are you sure?" Luci asked. Travis felt a little guilty.

"Yeah, I'm good. I've got snacks!" Hank flashed his teletab with the glowing credit at them and smiled.

"You two better get back in line." Hank added.

"We'll meet you just outside the gift shop?" Travis called back as he and Luci moved to the loading platform.

"Yep." Hank nodded.

He walked out the side gate and exited into the gift shop. Hank didn't want to admit it out loud, but he was actually relieved. The Vonderheist was a very, scary coaster. Hank was OK missing the Vonderheist.

Back in line, Travis and Luci were directed into a loading line at a fairly alarming rate. Once you made it past the scanner, there was no time to rethink your decision to get on the ride. They almost trotted up to the dock and a line of 'planes' pulled up and stopped. They hopped into a red and gold one, quickly strapping on the safety belts. An employee came along testing the devices. Luci noticed a mother in front of her holding her head in terror and resignation, sitting beside her exuberant child. Over the speaker, a woman's cheery voiceover echoed through the hanger repeating,

"Welcome Guest Pilots! Dr. Vonderheist and the MEEAD Research Center extend a most sincere thank you for testing our airships. We greatly appreciate your expertise in flight and navigation. If you should encounter any challenges, please use the 'eject' button, which is located at the center of the dash."

Luci looked down at the large 'eject' button and saw that it flashed 'error.' That was pretty funny.

The cars started moving slowly. Over the internal speakers in their plane there was a sudden microphone rumble and a male voice with a strong Chicago accent interrupted the voiceover.

"Wait! STOP THE TEST FLIGHTS! There is a geological disturbance on the island- an earthquake- the turbines are falling!"

Seemingly oblivious, the cheery woman's voice continues, *"Have a Safe Flight."*

Travis laughed, "There's no turning back now Luci. We're on this ride 'til the end. Hang tight."

Their plane jerked forward on the track with a jolt and shrieks of joy from the passengers filled the air as the plane thrust out of the hanger into the blue sky of Florida's Gulf. The coaster planes followed an inclining 'runway,' directed below by jumper clad animatronics waving directional lights. They climbed up the track of the first lift, rising above the park and Luci was mesmerized by the sheer beauty of it. From above, the Hovership almost looked like a compass, each direction was represented by a different color. The Vonderheist hanger and the runway was black, which must have indicated west. The train station in Amy Aime's had a yellow roof, Ma Ridgely's cafeteria was red and the Wrenaissance Theatre of Wonders was made of a faded, white washed tile. As they rose higher, they could see the air balloon of the Centrifuge with gondolas swinging almost vertical across the island.

Travis, who had ridden the Vonderheist many times before, knew what to expect, but he was still absolutely breathless at the dazzling view just at the top of the rise. The car hung in anticipation for almost 5 seconds, giving the passengers a chance to see over the edge of the park straight down to the coastal surf below them. It was liberating! Travis' favorite experience in the park- Luci was absolutely stunned, screaming in joy at the sheer breadth of it.

A brief flash of reflective light from the shadow of a hollow on Mt. Alta caught Travis' eye. Peering off in the distance (and honestly, he was a bit upside down) Travis was sure he saw someone off the path in the trees climbing up the face of the volcano. He focused on the figure, trying to see it clearly, just as the 'plane' let loose and plummeted straight down.

"What was that?" Travis's mind raced with the car as it sped up on the drop.

The coaster zipped down towards earth, swooping at the last minute around the hanger, to hug the curve as it roared over the wind turbine field. They felt themselves pulled into the seat of the car as the 'plane' twisted to avoid a spinning blade and headed into the loop. There was total weightlessness as they looped upside down, and plummeted back to the park, only to rise up again and dive toward a cement wall. A break appeared in the 'wall' (it is actually a hollow tower) and they lurched into it full speed and up. Leaving the tower, the plane lifted up, catching air on a series of hills and then took a curve, clinging to the outside bank and winding around another turbine.

The Vonderheist track swept out as if it was going off the edge of the park. As Travis and Luci swung out over the edge 'uncontrollably' they got another quick glance at the surf below them again. The coaster dipped down to avoid another bent turbine blade and then the plane found a straightaway over a pond. Suddenly, a 'gusher' rose up like a geyser and redirected them. The plane wove into and though the center of a tower as it shook and appeared to crumble around them. Rising again, they lifted out over the field, barely missing the tower wall, and lifted up through the turbines, winding into a final dip and then slowly stopped to finally dock at the hanger.

In three minutes it was over - but the adrenaline rush lingered. As they exited the ride into the gift shop, Luci was ecstatic, she couldn't talk enough about the view and the swooping and the screaming and - she just loved it. Travis smiled and talked too, but there was a nagging image that he couldn't shake. Just before the first drop, he remembered, he was sure he had seen a figure on the volcano.

8

Windy City Woes

Hank wandered out the door of the Vonderheist with a little less enthusiasm than he actually felt. (He didn't want Dustin and his thugs to think he was afraid to ride.) He casually walked over to the food truck across the plaza. It was early yet, but it was a good time for a snack. Hank was always hungry, breakfast was hours ago and it was going to be a long day. The windows to the truck were still closed, but Hank peered through the glass and spied a young man in a retro Cub's jersey who was just opening up the register.

"Can I get a slice?" Hank asked shyly. The truck sold Chicago pizza and hot dogs, sodas and salty snacks. The pizza looked fresh and delicious.

"I'm not really open, so I can't sell just yet." Stan the Cub's fan replied.

"Oh, sorry, I'll come back later." Hank started to step away, disappointed.

"It's OK, it's just the park won't let me process payment for another two minutes. I could slowly wrap up a slice just for you, my first customer of the day? It won't take long." Stan said. "If you're playing the park, there's an active key over to your left by the truck, where the line will be today. You can try and find it while you wait."

"Thanks" Hank smiled broadly and wandered off with his teletab, looking for a glowing bit in the 'parts' pile that was stacked up to mark a line, as yet unformed. The scrap included drift wood, a small brass ship's porthole, a rudder for a wing and a captain's wheel which glowed faintly as Hank approached.

"Cool." Hank collected the key and looked through his cache to see what he might put together. Just for fun. He was flipping through the screen, shuffling the keys and twisting them around when he heard the window slide open on the truck.

"Your breakfast is served!" The Cubs fan slid a slice out to Hank who swiped his teletab. The scan automatically paid for the pizza using Hank's snack credit. "Did you find the key?"

"Yes." Hank took a bite of the pizza and mumbled with his mouth full, "Thanks again for the tip."

"No problem. I'm glad it was there- Honestly, It's not always active- even this early in the morning. Its supposed to be but that key is one of George's favorites."

"What do you mean 'George's favorite'? I thought you could only collect a key once?"

"…If you're alive." Stan the Cubs fan grinned knowingly.

Hank gave him a blank stare.

"You haven't heard about George?"

Hank shook his head, slowly, suspiciously…chewingly.

Stan glanced around, gave Hank a conspiratorial look and lowered his voice. "You didn't hear this from me alright- look it up off park on your teletab- but George was one of the engineers here at the park. He was the real Cub's fan btw- the one responsible for arranging the franchise purchase? So, George had an accident before the park opened. One of the turbines fell on him before it was bolted down properly. He survived the accident, but was in traction in the hospital for two months. He actually finished some of the interactive components from the hospital bed. The day they stood him up at the hospital, a blood clot broke loose and killed him. It was really sad and shocking to everyone."

"Anyway, some of us run into him occasionally. Usually it's just folks talking about small things getting moved around. The keys get 'collected' before the park is open for instance. Just little things, that shouldn't happen normally. It may be a random glitch in the system, but we like to think its George looking out for us. I've even seen him once."

"Right." Hank wasn't sure what he was supposed to say to that. "Did you just say you've seen him?"

"Well, yes - once." Stan was looking at his watch anxiously. "I caught a glimpse of him leaning over the stack there as I came to work one day. It was cloudy. You know, sometimes the clouds here on the park are really dense until the surface temperature clears off the fog? So, I saw him in a spidery clearing. I know I saw something, because he stopped when he saw me, stared right at me and then took off into the fog. Also, the key was collected."

"Creepy." Hank was still doubtful.

"It's life on the Hoverpark." Stan laughed. "We're all working here together, to find the missing keys, fix the gadgets and save the world! Even the ghosts!"

While he was talking, a young couple walked up the window. "Well, its back to work for me- have a great day!"

"You too" Hank blurted out, but Stan the Cubs fan was already entertaining the next guests, serving up a slice and a story. It made Hank a bit more skeptical of the legend of George.

By the door of the Vonderheist Gift Shop was a DaVinci model flying machine, the aerial screw, which had a canvas sail that wound around like a cork screw. Hank was looking over a section of the aircraft when Luci and Travis came running out. Luci didn't really want to gloat about the ride so she toned down her excitement as they walked up.

"That's pretty impressive - I always like to imagine what it must have been like to explore something like flying."

"Painful" Hank laughed.

"Yeah, but think about it. They somehow knew we could, if they could just figure it out. It took true inspiration." Luci really loved the old artist inventors from back in the days when people studied arts *and* sciences together.

"Hey, get a photo for me will ya'?" Hank jumped up on the machine and handed his teletab to Luci. He sat in the wooden car under the sail and smiled big while Luci took the shot.

"How much are photo rights this year? Did you notice?" Hank asked as he took back his teletab. He looked at Luci who was oblivious and then at Travis who shrugged.

"What are you talking about?" Luci asked. The word 'rights' always got her attention.

"Hoverpark owns the rights to images in their park." Hank explained. "Any photos you take here get uploaded to their database and you purchase the rights to download them at the gift shop."

Luci rolled her eyes and shook her head in disgust.

"I'm going to buy the package." Hank smiled. He was surprisingly the nostalgic type. "I'll share them when we get home."

Luci nodded and gave him a little nudge. "You're a good egg Hank. Thanks for waiting for us."

"It's Ok… I got to hear this really great ghost story." He told them about George.

"That's pretty funny," Luci laughed. "High tech ghosts playing Hoverpark games."

"It's creepier, first thing the morning. Early morning fog makes everything creepier." Hank had to admit in the bright sun it did seem a bit silly.

"Ok, so where are we headed next?"

Travis had been silently musing on that question already. He hesitated and told them.

"Look, I saw something on Mt. Alta as we were on the Vonderheist. It looked like a person climbing the side of the Volcano."

"Maybe it was George." Luci offered grinning at Hank.

"Or maybe it was your guy Luci." Travis wasn't in a joking mood. Luci did this to him all the time. She'd point out something strange and then forget about it ten minutes later, depending on how she was feeling. He was left worrying about something Luci had already dropped.

"I'm pretty sure I saw our guy climbing up the side of Mt. Alta." Travis emphasized the 'our' and gave Luci a knowing look. "You saw someone break into the park."

"I *thought* I saw someone break into the park. You said so yourself, it was probably nothing." Luci defended herself.

"Well, I *know* I saw someone on Mt. Alta."

"I thought you weren't sure?" Hank was still in ghost mode.

"Look - Yes, I may be wrong, but it seems like two out of three of us have seen someone suspicious."

"And one of us is talking suspicious ghosts." Luci smiled and wiggled her fingers in evil hand jabs at Hank who glared back at her indignantly.

"I think we should try and figure out what is going on." Travis stood his ground. "It won't hurt to try."

"Alright, I'm just joking Travis." Luci continued, "I'm with you - and Hank is too." She grabbed Hank's hand and shook it weakly at Travis in agreement as Hank laughed embarrassed.

"Ok, here's the deal. I saw some guy climbing up the backside of Mt. Alta. It makes sense it might be the same guy Luci saw breaking past the bioscan into the park. We need to get back up in the air so we can see where he went. I think we should try to ride the Centrifuge. So let's head to the HoverLab, we can see the whole island from the Centrifuge and maybe we can catch him again."

Hank was not sure his slice of pizza was ready for the Centrifuge. "Isn't it still a little early to go spinning around in midair?"

"I thought you wanted to ride the Centrifuge?" Travis asked. He and Luci, were still on the adrenaline rush of the Vonderheist. For them, the Centrifuge was patty cakes.

"Well, we just got back here and by the time we get to the Centrifuge the lines will be Gy-normous!" Hank was feeling just a little queasy about spinning. His slice was definitely on the move. He really wanted to give his stomach a chance to settle.

"Come on Hank." Standing around was getting on Travis's nerves.

"Look, if you're so concerned, how about we tell security?" Hank said it. Travis and Luci looked at him in disbelief. But he'd said it and now there was no going back.

"Security, Hank? Are you out of your mind?" Luci was floored. She knew from experience that looking for security was ooking for trouble.

Hank held his ground. "It's what you should do, if you're- we're- worried that we might be in danger."

"No one said we're in danger Hank," Luci couldn't understand why anyone would want to engage authority. "We're just following up on a mystery - checking it out, so to speak."

"It sounds dangerous." Hank mumbled.

"Enough, already. Can we just travel? We can look for a security guard on the way." Travis was not really going to look for security, but he figured saying that was the best way to get Hank moving.

9

The Centrifuge

They walked past the Sue Namee Wave Pool in silence, with Hank stealing a lingering glance at the lounge chairs. They had barely stepped into Shell Plaza when Luci spotted a security guard. It was time to teach Hank a lesson.

"There, by the fountain, Hank. Lucky you, it's Officer Cy." Luci was the first to find him and she looked purposely at Hank who was feeling less and less enthusiastic about his idea. As emphasis, Luci actually crossed her arms and pointed with her chin.

"So - who's up for a little one -on-one with One-Eyed Cy?" Hank tried avoiding Luci's piercing eyes. How do girls do that? He wondered silently.

"That's rich! Get some gumption Hank, this 'Let's tell security plan' was your idea." Travis was not interested in chatting up Cy or even taking time to coax Hank to do it. He wanted to trail the intruder on his own. It was an adventure and they were wasting time.

Luci pushed Hank forward. "Go," She demanded.

Cyrus was glaring at them. Ominous and angry, he stood his ground like a vicious dog on a chain.

"Hello, Mr. Eye, I mean Cy, I mean Officer…" Hank looked at Cy's nametag, "Officer Pinter sir?"

"Yes." Cy looked around suspiciously and then re-focused on Hank standing in front of him.

"What do you want boy." Cy was not patient with students.

"Well, my friends and I, actually my friends saw something and we thought you should know…."

"If your *friends* saw something, why are *you* telling me?" Cy was not patient with anyone actually.

"Well, they sort of choose me to mention it to you, or rather someone, some security person, because you see sir, we saw a man climbing the volcano. He probably shouldn't be there."

At this point Travis, Hank and Luci's teletabs began buzzing. "Ms. Edison" Luci raised her hands in frustration, like this wasn't partially her fault. Travis affirmed their location and told Ms. Edison they were not in trouble. Their proximity to security was merely a question being asked.

"What question?" Ms. Edison conferenced. Travis could see his Mother's id slip into the conference.

"We saw someone suspicious. We're telling security." Luci added.

"That's ridiculous. You are to cease bothering park security immediately." Even Hank had to pull out his teletab which was responding with an emergency alert.

"If you do not stop this charade immediately, I will repeal your geotags."

"We're not joking," Hank started. Cy had taken the opportunity to step away from their 'game' and move onto something more security-like.

"No discussion." Ms. Edison continued. "Do you hear me? Apologize to security. I will be evaluating your activities every hour for the duration of our trip."

"What a jerk." Luci added to no one in particular as she watched Cy walk off. He could have at least tried to appear helpful. She felt a tad guilty. She just wanted to teach Hank no one took kids seriously. She was not happy about the additional monitoring. And she was a little sorry for being so rough on him. He was her friend after all.

"So now there's that." Travis said and looked at Hank and Luci neither of whom had much to say.

"Then it's agreed, we're going to the Centrifuge?" He added.

"Yes." Luci spoke for her and Hank.

"I'm sorry." Hank said. He'd done more damage trying to delay the centrifuge than the actual ride would have caused.

"It's OK Hank," Luci reassured him. "We'll have a great time on the Centrifuge and maybe the line won't be so long."

"I won't recommend talking to security again." Hank added. Luci gave him a reassuring pat on the back.

"He was a total jerk Hank." Honestly, it would have been helpful if Cy had taken at least a little bit of interest in the intruder. Even if she wasn't surprised, Luci didn't like being right about it either. And she was still feeling a little guilty.

The Centrifuge was located in Shell Plaza at the Hoverlab, just to the right of the entrance. It was an impressive draw for visitors, a towering series of swings that lifted from its base and rose 70 feet above the park to spin guests almost vertically out and over the other attractions. It was unrivaled in height and you could see everything, from the top of Mt. Alta, to the edge of the park.

The line to the Centrifuge was already enormous. Hank gave a deep sigh, but as luck would have it Travis noticed his Mom in the line. Penelope Pruitt was almost halfway through!

"Mom" Travis shouted joyfully. Luci crossed her fingers.

His Mom looked up, waved broadly and smiled. Catching on, she beckoned them boldly to join her asking, "Where've you been? Hurry now, I'm almost in the lab." The line wove guests through a series of outdoor experiments before entering the Hoverlab in a state of disarray from the volcano. Travis, Luci and Hank dodged between parkers, passing disgruntled, waiting, families to join his Mom in the line.

"Thanks" Travis muttered between his teeth as he caught up to her.

"You owe me." His Mom smiled.

"Thanks for holding a place for us Mrs. Pruitt." Hank blurted out, he was grateful but a bit shy to join them. Hank beamed sheepishly at the other people in line. It was a major violation, having someone hold your place in line…especially if you were faking it. People tolerated it if the saving involved children but three fifth graders were a bit much.

"You're welcome." Mrs. Pruitt added. "Now, what's this about a security question?"

"Mrs. Pruitt," Luci started, "Travis saw someone climbing the volcano."

"What?"

"There was a strange man climbing on Mt. Alta where he shouldn't be."

Penelope Pruitt dismissed the idea, "Well, I'm sure this man is just enjoying the park on his own. Not everyone comes with their family. The novelty of the park even existing is pretty exciting to some of us old folks."

"You're not old Mrs. Pruitt." Hank chimed in, grinning. Mrs. Pruitt gave him a sideways glance…Hank was a flatterer.

"Where are Tara and her friends?" Travis asked, changing the subject and willing Hank with his eyes to shut up.

"They're meeting me at the GENsys at 2:30. We're using our passes on that. They wanted to try the Vonderheist and I wanted to do this…You must have just missed them." Mrs. Pruitt wasn't distracted however, Travis was her son after all.

"You still haven't told me why security questioned you three of all people on this park."

"Ms. Edison has it backwards Mom. We went to security to tell them about the man." Travis explained.

"You're sure?" Mrs. Pruitt wasn't necessarily suspicious of them, but she knew Travis and it was not the first time that he had caused more than a little attention from law enforcement.

"I'm sure." Travis said indignantly.

"It's true Mrs. Pruitt. It was my fault." Hank added, always the defender of his friend. "I was the one that said we should tell security."

"Ms. Edison was not happy." Mrs. Pruitt added. "You should be more careful."

"Don't worry, we will." Luci said quietly.

"It was One-Eyed Cy." Travis said.

Mrs. Pruitt nodded, knowingly. "I don't want to have to baby-sit you three." All three of them nodded back in agreement.

"We won't be talking to Cy again anytime soon." Travis reassured her and Hank nodded emphatically.

The line brought them into the remnants of Dr. Wren's lab', where counters of broken equipment tottered into what appeared to be shattered glass on the floor. Old computers were cracked and shattered, circuits sparking. The floor was rived open and a geyser of steam and water poured into the lab. An open pipe hissed pink gas into the room and you could smell a slight hint of smoke. Almost instinctively, Luci turned a valve against the wall trying to shut off the pipe. Hank was a bit shocked at Luci's nerve- that she would reach out to touch one of the props. He was even more shocked when it worked. Instantly the valve began glowing, it was a key.

"Scan it Luci! It's another key!" Travis exclaimed.

Hank looked dejected. "I could have done that."

"You already have a valve key Hank. It's right there on your toggle, Travis pointed to Hank's utility belt where a toggle with a steam valve spun gleefully.

Hank shrugged sheepishly and Mrs. Pruitt gave him a gentle push.

"Congratulations Luci." He added.

"Thanks!" Luci was so excited she had hardly noticed. "This is actually fun you know." She said.

Travis smiled and Hank nodded. They knew.

As they left the lab and filed onto the loading dock, an audio track warned them.

"Aviators with heart, back or neck conditions should not join our flight today. This adventure is a fast paced free flight over the park. Do not attempt to ride this adventure if you are pregnant, dizzy

or have any underlying medical concerns that would be affected by heights or spinning."

They walked under what appeared to be an antiquated air balloon, brightly colored but faded over time. The basket in the center was not open for riding, but held an array of gears like complicated clockworks, and steam pipes riveted to what appeared to be a generator running the machinery. Steam emitted sporadically from the basket lifting the balloon ever so slightly in anticipated flight.

Underneath the balloon, their faces were reflected brilliant red, yellows and blues with shadows of black Victorian scrolling and flourishes. A boarding 'agent' directed each of them to individual gondolas parked along the outside of the balloon. Travis gave Luci and Hank a knowing look, reminding them to look for the intruder. Parkers were buckling into winged baskets, with wings reaching out from the center of each swing like a Jules Verne flying machine. One gondola had a bike pedal assembly just below it, and Travis quickly swept his teletab across it to collect the 'key.'

"Awesome Travis." Luci and Hank both congratulated him.

The actual mechanics of the Centrifuge were awe inspiring. Giant levers and gears began to turn slowly lifting the whole contraption up into air almost 70 feet high. The baskets were gently spinning as it rose. A blast of steam below gave the impression that their gondolas were being lifted up by an air current. They began to swoop and spin slowly, rising in ever increasing speed.

Just before the balloon reached its full height and began spinning faster, Hank suddenly looked back and pointed to a black dot moving stealthily through a hollow on Mt. Alta. Travis trained his eyes carefully in the direction Hank pointed to and saw a dark figure fiddling at something near the hydro electric dam. With a subtle clank, the balloon completed its accent, the wheels spun faster and each pod began lifting with centrifugal force until they were swinging out over the park in glorious free form.

"It's beautiful!" Luci shouted, distracted by the overwhelming view of the whole park.

The ride was spinning so fast the whole sky above them and the park below them was one enveloping blur. Penelope Pruitt yelled a loud hoot and Travis was reminded of what it must have been like for her, growing up competing in the Mt. Cloud Rodeo. His Mom was Ok, you know, for a Mom. The pods swept out and a portion of the edge of the Hoverpark blurred into view revealing a glimpse of the Gulf like an abyss below. They continued spinning for a good three minutes until the centrifuge began to slow down.

The 'balloon' began sinking back down to the dock and as the view cleared up, Travis glanced back over to Mt. Alta. He wasn't sure but he thought he saw someone in the bushes by the

Fracker flume. Quickly, he jerked his head back to get another look, but the gondolas were dangling below the balloon and the mechanics blocked his view. The carts docked and the safety doors unlatched. In front of him, Luci and Hank bounded out of their swing and all of them went tumbling out the exit.

"That was great!" Luci ran up to Travis.

"Did you see anything?" Travis asked.

"I actually forgot, sorry." Luci said, somewhat embarrassed.

Hank dashed up in excitement and started to tell Travis what he saw, but Travis quickly interrupted.

"Keep quiet and just smile for a minute." Travis looked from Luci and Hank to his Mom who was coming down the exit ramp towards them.

"What a rush! How'd you like it Luci?" Mrs. Pruitt loved sharing first experiences.

"It was brilliant!" Luci started. "You could see the curve of the park from up there, and if feels like you're flying over it."

"It does! I absolutely love it. Travis probably told you its one of my favorite rides here." She paused and looked around her at the beaming, youthful faces….guilty as all get out and laughed.

"Don't worry! I'm not going to follow you kids around." Penelope Pruitt grinned and gave them a passing wave, "I've got an early lunch date at La Ceiba with the girls."

When Penelope Pruitt said 'girls,' she meant she, Ms. Edison, Mrs. Nash and Mrs. Torez. La Ceiba was a café on Mt. Alta that overlooked the park where you could order drinks, salads, and appetizers like conch fritters. It was a favorite getaway for adults. The café looked like a Victorian spring, with 'natural' volcanic rock hot tubs, and cool pools surrounded by elegant tables and lounge chairs. It was very relaxing.

"Thanks, Mom. You're the best!" Travis chimed in a little sheepishly. Hank and Luci nodded in agreement.

"Really, Mrs. Pruitt. Thank you so much for letting us cut in, you saved us from a huge line."

"I'm glad I could share the ride with you. Now, you stay out of trouble, you hear?" Travis's Mom called back at them as she sauntered off to La Ceiba.

"Don't worry! Thanks again!" Travis, Hank and Luci all waved back at her and took off at a brisk pace.

10

Scheming

"Sorry 'bout that Hank." Travis apologized for cutting him off earlier. "We don't want Mom to hear or suspect."

"It's OK." Hank said.

"So what did you see?" Travis asked. Hank had definitely seen the intruder.

"I saw him on the mountain, by the waterfall where the Fracker flume drops, just above the hydro electric dam."

"That's what I saw too, but I couldn't tell what he was doing."

"Honestly Travis, It looked like he was pulling at a door or something."

"What is he up to? It seems like he knows the park pretty well." Luci added.

Travis nodded in agreement. He noticed that as well and he was more than a little interested in what the door was on Mt. Alta.

"Maybe he was trying to get into the volcano. It could be an entrance into the cave?" Travis grinned a little. "I'd like to know if it was an entrance door - who's up for an adventure?"

They were standing on a little bump out over the Gad About River, looking at Mt. Alta and mentally trying to figure out the location of the door.

"I think it was up there, beside that tree - it looks like a live oak." Hank pointed.

"If I travel between the Fracker flume and the dam, I should be able to find it." Travis said.

"Travis! You can't go wandering off on the park, Ms. Edison will know." Luci was afraid to miss her only day on the Hoverpark.

While Luci and Travis bickered, Hank wandered to the edge of the bump out to look out over the Gad About River. He could see just the edge of the Sue Namee swimming hole and the Blue Holes playground. A series of aqua ducts carried water across the playground and sprayed young kids splashing along in puddles below. A child was turning the water screw bringing water up into a basin that dumped onto unsuspecting victims. An older child was rolling the tread wheel, bringing water up into the main pool. Two boys were lifting a large bucket of water with a series of pulleys like a ship's block and tackle. A group of girls were moving through a canal maze, shifting water levels to reveal fantastic creatures, tunnels and colorful tiles.

As Hank watched the kids, Mt. Alta began rumbling, steam emitted from the top and an alarm went off alerting the younger kids in the Sue Namee wave pool. In a giant swoosh; larger waves began sweeping through the pool as screams of joy wafted up toward the volcano. Then the Fracker tossed a cart down the flume toward the dam, and it made the whole scene of chaos and thundering waves complete. It was almost surreal how perfect it was…the screaming adults, the squealing kids and the unstable volcano rumbles. It looked positively wonderful. If Hank had his way, they'd be hitting the water now. Well, maybe after a little snack or at least a taste of something.

Luci and Travis joined the edge of the bump out with Hank as he looked out over the dam. They were still bickering over their next move.

"Travis, we're going to lose our geotags if we continue following this guy."

"There's nothing that says we can't go to the Fracker and ride it."

"Yes, but we're not supposed to be exploring random doors… and you know you will."

"We can't just let him go into Mt. Alta Luci - someone has to stop this guy."

"But that someone doesn't have to be you."

"I was thinking more like 'us' actually." Travis made his best attempt at looking wounded.

"No. It's not worth it. Let's just have fun."

"This is fun! Aren't you just the slightest bit interested in that door? He's long gone by now, I just want to find the door. Don't you want to know what he was doing?"

"You're not going to let this go are you?"

"Well, the Fracker is on our list. It's not going to hurt to go now."

Luci rolled her eyes and looked at Hank up against the low wall over the river. She'd lost the argument. Honestly, it wasn't much of one to begin with. She did want to know what the intruder was up to. They didn't have to open the door, they could just find it. Also, Travis was good at the bait and switch - they did want to go on the Fracker and she couldn't think of a good enough reason not to go on it now.

Knowing he'd won, Travis moved forward. "The quickest way to Mt. Alta is to the left, back through Ma Ridgley's courtyard." He was excited and ready to roll.

"Seriously, Travis?" Hank started dragging along behind them. "Have we honestly walked all the way around the park once already?" Hank was beginning to wear down a little. It was late morning, his slice at the Vonderheist was long gone and he was beginning to feel a little weak in the knees.

"Not quite." Travis mumbled. There was no reason to rub it in. "Come on Hank, we're going to the Fracker! You wanted to ride it more than once remember?"

After being reminded that it was his ride of choice, Hank perked up a bit. They could have lunch after the Fracker. Or he could get a snack at the gift shop. There was plenty of time to do the Gad About. And it will be warmer later on in the afternoon. A perfect plan, if he didn't say so himself.

They were just on the other side of the bridge and starting to head up Mt. Alta when suddenly a section of the rock wall started glowing.

"Whoa!" Luci stopped and admired the wall. "Guys, did you see this?"

"Holy Crap!" Hank's teletab was activated, with tickertape flashing and his personal theme music playing. Elated, he flipped through his keys. Travis tried to advise him and Luci was looking over his shoulder fascinated.

"Try that block of three pulleys Hank, I'm pretty sure you can make a crane...."

"Stop it Travis. It's my portal. Let me play it." Hank wanted to create his own glory. What use was a toggle if someone else created it for you?

"Sorry dude, I just got excited." Travis stepped back so Hank could think.

"I think a crane is a good idea though." He said glancing back at Travis who smiled and nodded.

Hank held up his teletab to the glowing rocks. The rock face suddenly melted into itself as a portal opened. The portal was just large enough to allow Hank to enter the small cave like room surrounded by activated ether screens. Luci and Travis watched from outside the portal in the sunlight as a glass door closed behind him. They could see as Hank stepped up to screens and started manipulating the keys. Each of his keys loaded onto the screens like puzzle pieces, and a timer began ticking very quietly. With sweeping motions Hank pulled out the block of three pulleys and a wooden frame like an easel and connected them to a winched bar.

Two pieces started glowing almost immediately but the block of pulleys was still a cool blue on the screen. Travis could barely contain himself, he tried to tell him but the teletab contact was broken inside the portal. Hank moved the block of pulleys around trying to figure out what was wrong. The once quiet ticker was becoming louder and louder in the room room. It almost sounded like the pounding of Hank's heart, urging him forward. Finally, Hank noticed the arrows on the pulleys and arranged them so the line would run smoothly through the top. The object started glowing and flashing a warm orange. For some reason, the Captain's wheel glowed purple on the side, though Hank's crane was obviously done.

"You did it Hank!" Luci was mesmerized.

"You haven't seen the best part," Travis murmured under his breath. And almost on cue, the whole portal began celebrating.

The sound of music, flashing lights and applause accompanied the opening of a small niche where an elegant blueprint appeared. The blueprint crane began moving, in brilliant color while a 3-D printer began laying recycled plastic layer by layer until a toggled badge grew complete on the tray. As the toggle cooled, red lights began circling the tray until finally all the lights in the portal shut off, the tray opened and in the glow of red lights lay a brand new toggle.

Hank reached for it with pride and slipped the toggle onto his utility belt as he stepped out into the sun. The darkened portal closed behind him, leaving the appearance of a solid rock face. If he didn't have the new toggle, Hank would not have believed it himself.

"I want - actually, I need to do that." Luci stated with conviction. "How many keys do I have to collect? Where is the next portal? What about that crane, can I make that. Where did you get the parts Hank? Travis?"

Hank laughed, he didn't always get to enjoy this kind of glory. Travis tried to slow Luci down a little. Hank knew that was futile, but it was fun to watch.

"Relax Luci, your best strategy is just to collect as many keys as you can and figure it out when a portal opens. You can't make the same toggle. Sometimes, you can but the system is fighting the copying. I don't know how, maybe it's through geotags? But trust me; you will not be able to make a crane today - even if you collect the same keys."

"No. I don't accept that." Luci kept on. "You have a lot of toggles Travis; I know you know how to do this. Tell me what to do or I am going to get very upset."

"I did tell you Luci." Travis continued, "Just keep collecting keys. Any key you find. The more keys you have, the more you likely you are to have the right ones."

"When you have the right parts, a portal will open." Hank added. "Travis is right Luci. He can't give you the answers, because the game keeps changing."

"I have a valve and an old wing? What kind of invention will that make? Is there any rhyme or reason to this game? Can't I just go find the parts I need?"

"Yes, but you'll drive yourself nuts. Just look through your cache and think about what you have. If you realize something important is missing, Tara says you can figure it out sometimes." Travis didn't understand why girls always had to feel like they had control over the world.

"Come on guys, let's go. There's no reason to stand here. Hank has already completed this portal." Travis added.

Hank just beamed. Luci reluctantly left the portal.

"You can go ahead and choose your theme music though," Travis added, "If you want something different from your usual teletab settings."

Luci smiled at that and set her theme song while they walked. It made her feel ready. She couldn't wait.

"All this excitement has made me a bit hungry." Hank chimed in again on a suggestion for a snack. Or lunch. Why not? It was after 11 and it wasn't like the Fracker was going to close down any time soon.

11

Ma Ridgley's

As they rounded the corner back to Ma Ridgley's Courtyard, Luci started pointing out some of the funny puns and little hidden word games she found scattered throughout. She was much more impressed this time around with the guest services sign which was a handwritten 'guest' over the 'service entrance' door, and an added 's' after 'service'. The mop and pail beside the door, just added to the whole effect.

The smell of Ma Ridgely's cafeteria was wafting over the courtyard, drawing them in. Hank started to mumble something along the lines of 'good time for a snack' but he didn't have to say much more. Travis and Luci easily began circling round the menu board. It was a good time for lunch. The choices included: Home-a-Sassy Salad, Ybor City Cuban Sandwiches and Florida BBQ.

The cafeteria was a cross between a diner and a beach hut with walls of scrap wood and a palm roof. It was homey and familiar, with 'vintage' photos of Ma Ridgely; one along the beach holding a lobster in each hand, one presenting a homemade Key Lime Pie and one celebrating with the MEEAD Center staff and scientists at an outdoor cookout. In the corner was a glass fridge with 'a gallileon' of milk. There were pastries shaped like an 'L' called Buns 'L's. Luci was thrilled when she realized a scale on the counter read a 'ton' and the little lizard looking animal resting on a block of ice on the scale was actually a 'newt' making the whole thing a pun.

"Look guys, 'Newt Ton' it says Newton, wait - Iced Newt - Isaac Newton, that's hilarious!" Luci pointed it out. Travis had never noticed it before. That's why he liked Luci.

Ma Ridgely's staffers behind the plates of food wore classic aprons in a variety of red patterns and each one tried to convince the guests to add an impulse purchase of healthy options - oranges, apples, bowls of strawberries and a tray of whole carrots. Comments like, "You really should try a carrot 'teen' they're good for you, lots of vitamin A" or "You know what they say, an apple a day". Along the wall behind them were Old Florida nature paintings of roseate spoonbills, crocodiles and Florida panthers. There were also more framed photos and newspaper clippings of MEEAD center events, ranging from Thanksgiving celebrations, a 4th of July clambake, and a birthday party for a smiling Amy complete with vegetable kabobs and a cake decorated like a giant bee.

The BBQ was an easy choice for Hank and Travis, though Luci went with the 'Madame Vegetable Curry' and rice instead. Travis loved strawberries, so he ended up with a bowl of them to share. They carried their meals to a table by the fountain.

"What is this stuff?" Hank was picking at the greenish wrapper of his sandwich.

"It's edible," Travis answered. "Though I wouldn't try it. It tastes nasty, but the bugs like it. It biodegrades really fast - only takes a couple days."

"I read about it…." Luci looked closer at the wrapper and collected it with her teletab as a tagged artifact. It flipped into her online field journal, and she took a few notes, talking the whole time. "They make it out of gelatinous plant fibers. All the packaging here on the park is made of it - so they can compost it on site instead of shipping it down through the conduits to the surface."

"Smart." Hank shrugged and tossed it to the side. "The barbeque is good."

There was the relaxed quiet of eating, well almost quiet. Hank had a bad habit of smacking as he wolfed his sandwich down.

"I just can't believe someone can wander loose through the park like this." Luci said out loud to no one in particular.

"At least it's just one guy, not like the Orlando attack..." Travis volunteered. Hank and Luci stopped talking and looked at Travis meaningfully. He never talked about Orlando.

"You were there weren't you?" Luci asked quietly. It was a rhetoric question. Luci already knew the answer.

"Yeah, but I don't remember much. My Dad got us all off one of the rides which was burning. I remember having to jump over the track. Actually what I remember is falling after trying to jump over the track, but I'm told that's not what happened, so I'm not the best witness."

"What does your Dad say happened?"

"Well, you know, he's not around anymore. In fact, he left us shortly afterward, and kind of disappeared...we don't really know where he is. Not even Mom. But Mom said the fire tore through the attractions quickly after the explosions. The confusion was the biggest problem. They had a great evacuation plan, but they needed leaders to help guide people.

What happened is, the cell towers and utilities were taken out in the blasts and so communications were spotty. Since they attacked all of the parks, there was a lot of chaos. Emergency vehicles didn't know where to go because there were multiple locations in parks all across Orlando. On the rides, if there wasn't a manager right there, no one knew what to do. The staff members were completely confused and many of the tourists evacuated themselves. Mom says that once we got out of the ride into the main park, the evacuation went smooth and that was what really helped."

Luci nodded. "I heard the fires on the rides were the worst part it. I noticed they have fire brands here - everywhere- so anyone can grab one and use it."

"Yeah, that's smart. The fire in the ride was awful. The smoke was so thick you couldn't see anything except the burning sets. We were taking service walkways, but we didn't know the exits. So instead of being able to use a door or evacuation exit, we had to walk back out towards the front, towards the entrance and exit. There were only a few staff members, and most of them were not old enough to really help. One guy was there for me though, so I can't really complain."

Hank and Luci watched Travis, silently waiting. Travis reluctantly continued,

"My Dad, Mom and Tara were on the other side of the track. We were trying to walk out together you know, in tandem, but there was a fire blocking the walkway on my side and I couldn't continue. Dad yelled for me to jump over the track, but it was pretty scary. Anyway, I didn't really commit in the jump so I tripped and fell. I had one hand on some vines which were ripping off the wall. This young guy reached out and caught me. He grabbed me by my belt and swung me up over to my dad. At least that's what I'm told. Like I said, all I actually remember is falling. The Doctor says that is an invented memory. Its funny,

I also remember this sort of angry face which I always thought was an animatronics pirate. His wrist had a red spider on it? I'm not sure what that is about? Maybe it was a tattoo? It's weird, you know, the silly things you remember as a kid."

Luci and Hank nodded.

"My folks talk about the Orlando attack sometimes." Hank chimed in so Travis wouldn't feel quite so put on the spot. "They used to work in the parks when they were kids, so they still knew a lot of people who were there when it happened. They said there was this one guy, who entered the burning rides and helped injured guests escape, one after another. He was personally responsible for saving around 36 people, and when others saw him they were inspired to join the effort. That's how hundreds of people were evacuated from some of the worse areas."

Travis added. "It was pretty amazing. We were lucky. On our ride there were only a few casualties. One mother and her child were in a car way in the back, and they couldn't make it out on the walkways before the flames engulfed the whole building. She had to carry the kid and it slowed her down a lot. He was only a year old. She was pretty young too; at least that's what the media said."

Luci was horrified. She knew a little about Travis' family, but didn't realize they were actually one of the survivor families. "I'm surprised you come to the park at all," She asked, almost to herself.

"It's not that big a deal really. Things have changed, and security is better. I do pay closer attention to the exits though. And I'm great at hidden doors!" Travis laughed. "…Well, almost great." He was still flustered by the door he saw on Mt. Alta.

"We'll find it, Travis." Luci reassured him. "I'm not guaranteeing we'll actually be able to use it, but we'll find it!"

"Don't worry Travis. You'll get into Mt. Alta - one way or another!" Hank added smiling and tapping his toggles. Travis only had one more toggle to go and he should get the Game Master cave tour. In silence, all three of them almost dozed off in the speckled shade of a live oak, dripping with Spanish moss. A ladybug crawled along the edge of the table. And Luci looked up to see a dragon fly flit across the nearby pond.

12

Mt. Alta

"Are you guys done yet? Nap time is over, it's time to go." Travis said. Rejuvenated, he roused Hank and Luci from their food coma with a bold reminder of their mystery. "We've got a door to find!"

Travis led them across the bridge, over the Gad About River to Mt. Alta. As they walked across the bridge, below them kids and parents were lounging about in inner tubes and rafts, relaxing and going where the current took them. On one side of the river, a round target like a donut of stone was set up and boys were trying to toss beach balls through the center hole as they floated by. From the bridge you could just make out the edge of the 'Cenote,' a clear bottomed pool nestled along Mt. Alta that gave swimmers a bird's eye view of the surf below them.

"Look there" Luci pointed, "It's that same Mom and kid we rode up with on the elevator!"

"Where?" Travis asked. There were so many people it was hard to see.

"Over by the 'Eye of Horus' carving in the wall…see them? Now, they're passing that dancing figure…" Luci's voice trailed off as she tried to describe the hieroglyphics they were passing as they floated down the river. Finally, Travis recognized the Mom and kid floating in an inner tube spinning slightly as they bounced against the stone like walls.

"It's funny, how that happens." Travis responded. "I never see my friends when I come to the park, but I usually run into the same group of people all day long. I don't know why - it's not like we're even on the same rides."

"Speaking of friends," Hank pointed out an aggressive group of boys splashing and making a general nuisance of themselves as they floated alongside families. Dustin and his friends Tosh and Melvin were spreading theirs special obnoxious joy amongst the masses. It was like watching a group of people separate around a rabid dog. The mass of lazy river floaters broke up around Dustin and his friends giving them ample space to splash and terrorize each other.

As they watched Dustin and his crew float away, Hank mumbled, "What a way to waste away the day!" He looked wistfully at the lazy river, and glanced at Luci, but she wasn't having it. Luci was ready for a new adventure and Travis was already across the bridge on Mt. Alta. He was pacing by the open rock face.

On the other side of the bridge was an open cut in Mt. Alta where a series of climbing walls were carved out in various types of rock. As they walked past, Travis, Hank and Luci started collecting objects along the path.

"Check it out-Oolitic Chert!" Travis tagged a rock face.

"What is that?" Hank tagged the wall as well.

"The little round circles are the fossilized shells of 'oolites' or little creatures. It makes the rock look polka dotted."

"Look a trilobite!" Luci was collecting fossils in the crevasses of a shale rock. Little bits and pieces were scattered around the ledge where children were locking their feet on the way up the wall.

"And a graptolite…" Travis was holding a little piece of shale with what looked like a twig in it.

"I found a shell" Hank chimed in; he was pleased to have another object tagged.

"Check out the zip line…" Luci was developing a growing interest in the climbing wall. Kids were attached to harnesses and climbing up the side of the wall. As they reached the top, you could take a small zip line down and either drop off into the Cenote or dismount on a dock. A small flight of stairs lead to a lookout over the Cenote. The wooden deck came complete with lounge chairs and a tiki bar serving drinks and snacks and sandwiches. A young girl in pig tails came running up to her dad, her whisper wick suit was dry by the time she reached him, and she gave him a big hug and asked if she could go again. Dad, who was comfy in the shade with a beer and banana chips, said, "Yes, honey." No surprise there.

The area at the center was crowded. It was partially blocked by parkers, standing in the middle of the path. Parkers, confused about where to go next, would suddenly come to a complete stop with their stroller and pulled out their teletabs- completely oblivious to the fact that there were people walking behind them. Tara liked to call them 'traffic zits.' By mistake, Travis brushed against a man weaving deftly through the crowd, going in the opposite direction. The man was alone, probably waiting for his kid to come down from the wall.

"Sorry." Travis murmured, looking back at the man's shoes. They were a heavy for the park, black and skid free which was a bit dorky.

"Nice toggles" The man said, surprising Travis.

"That one is very rare. Only about four people have completed that puzzle."

He pointed to the water mill toggle. It was Travis's fifth toggle and in fact, one of his favorites. He'd never met anyone else who had one.

"Thanks." Travis looked down to admire it, "I solved it last year." but when Travis glanced back up the man was gone. He had completely vanished. He tried to shrug it off, but it nagged at him. How did he know only four people had solved that puzzle? Travis was a fanatic about toggles, but this guy seemed weirder than your average toggler. Travis had a feeling the incident would come back to haunt him.

Luci, in the meantime, had found the entrance to the Fracker. "Over here guys." She was fairly giddy about flume rides and moved so fast to get into line that she almost ran face first into Officer Cy. Backing up quickly, she apologized (for going in the right direction!) Cy Pinter glared and tried to look authoritative, but he didn't stop. He was obviously in a hurry.

"Better watch your step." Travis said to Luci pointing to his teletab. They didn't want to risk alerting Ms. Edison. That whole 'next to security' thing was completely unfair.

The line for the Fracker wound around and around in a zig zag, beginning near the climbing wall.

"Ugh…" Hank moaned. It was an hour long at minimum.

"We'll use our line pass." Travis decided for everyone. It was a bit bossy, but Luci and Hank went with it.

Even the line pass line was long, taking them around the edge of Mt. Alta to a wooded hollow deeply shadowed and mysteriously quiet. Whimsical signage along the path warned everyone 'for evil scientists only' and you could hear a deep rumbling regularly punctuated with screams from the volcano, it was ominous and added to the anticipation in the line. A 'secret' passageway in a large 'cement' block carried the line indoors bypassing many of the people. To enter, they waved their teletab pass at a scanner which appeared to be scanning their face. A gate opened, giving them passage into the front of the existing line. Through a crumbled wall they could see the sparking of two Tesla coils in the next room resonating and flashing to ethereal music.

Luci laughed "Now you know we're entering the lab of an evil mastermind intent on taking over - or destroying - the world!"

Travis and Hank looked at her puzzled.

"Tesla coils? Come on guys, I'm guessing the next room will be a closet of black turtlenecks?"

The guys shook their head as Luci laughed. She was having fun. And when they turned the corner into the next room, Luci uttered a resounding, "Yes!"

It was an evil scientist playroom, with all the props and toys a budding mad scientist could ever want! One touch screen of the world featured missile launch buttons - in glowing red. Along the wall was a caged cell for 'interfering' do-gooders. The left side of the map had faded away revealing an interior room completely covered with blueprints, digital gadgets and complicated mathematical formulas. As the line continued, they passed an upright cast iron gurney on a lever positioned precariously below a sparking ray gun. Luci jumped in front and had Hank take a picture for her.

"What do you think? Do I make a good nemesis? I'm going to be the stoic vengeful type." Luci offered a stiff resisting glare for the photo.

Together, they caught up with Travis who was sliding a magnetic North around the world map on a magnetic polar shift simulator. As the north changed, it altered the shape of the world's continents and ocean; flooding and shifting the general world. "Check it out" Travis laughed, "….Florida, no Florida, Florida, no Florida."

The line wove out of the room into a dark hall where a series of buttons allowed you to unleash holographic saw blades, spikes, snakes and fireballs on other guests. They walked across a grate on the floor. Below them alligators snapped and sharks circled as the crowd slowly formed a neat queue and began winding through an abandoned hall, with industrial piping weaving along the ceiling. The room echoed with the clangs of loud hydraulic pumping. The sounds pounded all around them and shook the interior which periodically sprung a leak. The whole experience, while manufactured as part of the ride, still inspired certain fear among the guests. Signs hanging precariously along the walls added to the effect, "Protected by Death Ray," and "None of your beeswax, Amy."

Around a corner, the line began climbing a flight of metal stairs up to a loading platform and they could see parkers boarding a flume shaped like a metal submarine cut in half. Staff in lab coats directed them into a glass bottomed boat of rivets and bubbled portholes, in short, a Jules Verne design that intensified the sense of mishap. When their turn came, Travis, Luci and Hank were able to ride on one bench, the three of them together, in the front of the ship with about five more benches behind them. A boy in a clean white lab coat raised his arm as he manipulated a control panel. With a small jolt, they were launched and the boat inched along a waterway going deeper into the warehouse.

The flume slowly circled around the dim cement lab, passing hydraulic pumps, tubes and turbines. There was the sound of slamming and pounding deep in the mountain. They couldn't help but feel like they were somewhere they shouldn't be - and as they rounded the corner, flashing red lights and emergency strobes emitted alarms along the ceiling. A burning electronic control panel filled the room with smoke. Buttons flashed and sparked and loose wires hung dangerously close to the water. The flume circled round the pump, the pipes bulging, as the metal started to burst open at the rivets, revealing smoking gears. They floated through this second room as it started to buckle. Suddenly, there was darkness.

In the bottom of the flume (which now had emergency lights) they saw the stream bubbling. A fissure burst open and all around them was heated steam and the gargling of water. Voices shouted over the alarms.

"We need to release the pressure, get them out of there, Open the gates, OPEN THE …."

The flume slid past magma oozing along the room's corners into the bright light of the outdoors. In a loud swoop, the wall in front of them 'crumbled' to reveal a precipice and opened fissures, in the warehouse. Out they flow. The edge of the building overlooked the hydroelectric dam, 80 ft. below.

As the flume reached the edge of the precipice, the volcano seemingly rose around them and for a short moment, they had a beautiful vista of the park from Mt. Alta. Below them, the turbines of the hydroelectric dam were spinning and waves began building around them. The flume slowly inched towards the drop, water sloshing over the sides as it picked up speed and dropped toward the spinning turbines below. Then - without warning - the ride stopped! The sloshing water began receding. For a brief moment there was confusion. Why aren't they falling? Luci thought. Poised over the precipice, they noticed the water behind them has stopped boiling, and the water below them is draining to reveal a hooked track. The creaking and explosive sounds are still going on but the bursting geysers have all stopped.

"What's happening?" Hank stated the obvious as the lights behind them came on. The Fracker had come to a complete stop.

"Hang in there" Travis said. (He didn't realize what he'd said until Hank and Luci started laughing.)

By the time they'd stopped chuckling and started looking around again, Luci had her teletab out and was consulting the map.

"Guys, the Fracker is listed as down on the map. They're advising people to find other rides."

Travis sighed. It appeared the Fracker wasn't going to start up again any time soon.

13

Fractured

As Travis, Hank and Luci waited in their flume, a loud voice came over the intercom to reassure them. "*Please remain seated. Evacuation of the Fracker is currently in progress and a staffer will be with you shortly. Please remain seated. Evacuation of the Fracker is currently in progress and a staffer will be with you shortly. Please remain seated.*" It was a loop.

Behind them, guests were being instructed by staffers, to step out of the flumes and exit along the service route. Below them, Travis, Hank and Luci could see special equipment being brought in to evacuate the flumes in the water. It was an interesting process, while the water on the flume is only a few inches deep, a special set of stairs is brought in to help guests exit without slipping.

Perched on the precipice overlooking the drop, Travis, Luci and Hank could see past the hydro electric dam into the Sue

Namee wave pool. The pool was quiet and still, and the surface was like glass since all the people had been evacuated out of the water. From where they were sitting, they could see through the clear bottom of the pool. It was designed with a section of it 'open' so guests could leave the safety of a false coral reef and if they were looking down, it would seem like floating in the sky - like they were flying. Watching the running children on the beach below, Travis realized he was missing a great opportunity. The door they were trying to find was just a short way through the hedge on the left!

"I'm going to investigate guys. You stay here, I'll be back shortly." Travis flung his legs over the flume.

"Where are you going!" Hank was shocked.

Luci too was alarmed at Travis' total lack of regard for his own safety.

"Travis, what are you doing? The track might be electrified. You can't just get off like that!"

Luci's voice trailed off when it became apparent that obviously he could. The track wasn't electrified, it was magnetic. But an alarm went off alerting the staff that someone had left the cart. Luci shrugged. There wasn't much she could do at this point.

"No time to explain, I gotta go !" As he walked off he yelled, "I'm pretty sure the door we saw is just over the bushes there to the right." Travis pointed. At the top of the small hill, he stopped, turned and added, "I'll meet you at the exit. Don't worry."

Hank looked at Luci for support but she just smiled weakly and shook her head.

"What are we gonna do? It's Travis. He'll be fine, I'm sure of it. He's always fine." Luci said.

Dodging into the bushes, Travis glanced back to see Luci talking and pointing at something. He watched her count on her fingers as she gestured in the direction of the Vonderheist. He laughed a little and pushed through the other side of the hedge finding a narrow path that trailed along the rock face just above the hydroelectric dam. Travis started jogging along the path, keeping his eyes open for staff. Remembering how easy it was to spot the intruder, he hunkered down low trying to keep below the bushes. In the distance, he heard voices and jumped into the brush. Creeping slowly forward, he saw a small clearing and several men arguing at a metal door, which was opened to reveal an open circuit board.

Travis was disappointed at first, thinking he'd gone to all this risk just for nothing. Listening in, he heard the men arguing about the repairs.

"It's burned I'm telling you. Look at that - have you ever seen a fuse short out from a fire that started on the outside?"

"I think that's just flames from the fire inside."

"Are you blind? I've been doing this for years, and I'm telling you this fire started on the outside."

"Geez Mike, does it matter? Just get the pliers will ya'? We need this board running as soon as possible."

The workman named Mike, cursed a bit and stepped over to the path where a tool box was lying open on the ground just in front of Travis. Travis tried to take a step back hiding further into the leaves, but his foot got caught on a rock and he tripped falling backwards, snapping twigs and branches. Mike almost jumped out of his skin.

"What the…?" he leapt up and poked his head over the brush to see Travis, still lying on the ground looking sheepish.

"Hey kid, what are you doing here?"

"I just heard voices so…" Travis started talking and thinking at the same time. What was he going to say? He was saved by the bullish Mike interrupting him.

"You're not supposed to be here. Get up and get out of those bushes."

Mike stood looking at him for a moment then he grabbed Travis by the arm a little roughly and demanded, "Did you have anything to do with this fire?"

Travis was suddenly terrified. He hadn't thought of that outcome!

"No" he blurted, "No Sir." He tried to act as innocent as he could. "I was on the Fracker and just wanted to see what had happened. I was on the other side of the bushes. I was just curious how long it would take when I heard you guys over here. I knew I shouldn't be here. I was just looking. I'm sorry."

Mike looked at Travis closely. He scowled angrily and looked into his eyes. Travis could tell he was trying to see if he was lying and he looked back at him as innocently as he could. Suddenly, Mike let go.

"You aren't smart enough." He said in disgust. Travis rubbed his arm a little, trying to look calm.

"Hey Fred - over here. Look what I found" Mike called over to one of the other workmen. One man, obviously 'Fred' reluctantly left the group and slowly came up to where Mike was standing. He looked surprised to see Travis.

"Listen kid, Fred here is going to take you back."

"Thank you, sir." Travis was anxious to get back to the main park. His teletab was buzzing with a question mark from Ms. Edison.

"My teacher, sir, she wants to know where I am."

"Well, you'd better tell her then." Mike turned and nodded to Fred who started walking up another path to the right, beckoning Travis to follow him.

"Come on kid."

"Travis walked and typed back to Ms. Edison "Just evacuating a ride that was shut down." The teletab was quiet for a moment. Then Ms. Edison typed back "Strike two. I'm watching you Travis."

Travis was a bit stumped on how the teletab knew he was not where he should be. Maybe Luci was right about this big brother stuff.

"Come on kid, Lets go. I got work to do."

Travis followed Fred quietly until he figured he might try to ease the silence with some small chat. "So, what happened?" He asked.

"Nothing happened." Fred barked back. And then he added, "A short circuit on the door there caused the power to go out. We're going to need some time to fix it so we're evacuating the ride. It happens. No big deal."

Travis looked down at the Gad About where people were waiting by the docks and the floats were bobbing empty in the pool. "What about the Gad About?" He asked.

"It's the same circuit. When something goes wrong, water control shuts down all the gates so the water doesn't flow. It's a safety precaution. We'll have it up and running again in no time. We just need to repair the circuit and run a safety check. In fact, we'd probably have it running already if it wasn't for your meddling."

Travis took the hint and remained quiet for the rest of the walk, which was short. The path ended at a short unlocked gate. Travis went through the gate and turned to thank Fred, but he'd already headed back up the path.

14

Try, Try, Again

Travis found Hank and Luci by the entrance to the Fracker sitting on stools made to look like 'turbines' around a gear table. They were anxiously looking at the side of Mt. Alta and were visibly relieved to see Travis.

"Well?" Luci and Hank asked Travis, waiting for him to tell them what he found.

"It was just a circuit box. Not a door at all." Travis was visibly disappointed about the door but still excited about what he learned.

"I sort of snuck up on some workmen trying to fix a circuit breaker. I'm guessing that's why the ride is down? They were arguing about it. Anyway, they found me in the bushes, so that wasn't fun. Some guy named Mike grabbed me and Ms. Edison called."

"You seek this kind of trouble out Travis." Luci blurted out, she couldn't help herself.

"It's OK. I told her we were being evacuated from a ride and she bought it. Anyway, this old guy Mike actually thought I had messed with the box, but then he backed off. He had another guy walk me out to the gate and I found you. But here's the deal - I'm guessing our intruder pried open the box, thinking he was opening a door. He must have given up when he realized it was just a circuit box and gone on to look for another door!"

"Seriously, Travis? Are you even hearing yourself?" Luci asked. "What makes you think he's trying to find a door?"

"What else would he be looking for on the side of Mt. Alta?"

"How about a circuit box?"

"Pfft - What's the point of that?" Travis was just sure this intruder was trying to get inside.

A light buzzing lit up their teletabs and Hank looked down with delight, "Look guys, the ride is back up and we got replacement passes. Let's go!"

"But didn't you hear what I just said? We need to find out where the intruder went, maybe he found another door." Travis really wanted to find the doorway into Mt. Alta.

"Are you kidding me? Did you see that drop we missed? This ride has to be fabulous when it's working!" Luci added, "Let's try it again!"

"I'm game, let's go." Hank agreed without a blink.

"But we're supposed to be looking for the intruder." Travis protested.

Luci stopped in her tracks and turned around.

"No Travis. We're supposed to be enjoying the park. Yes, we saw something weird, but now, you've taken off on this wild goose chase. We don't even know this is the same guy! Let me do the math for you Travis, you've got two strikes on your geotag, you're wanting to go find someone who may or may not exist, and now you don't even know where to go. What is wrong with you?" Luci was losing patience.

"Me? I thought we were all in on it?" Travis was starting to get defensive.

"We are - or were - or maybe we still are," Luci halfheartedly agreed, "but we also want to have fun. And the trail has run dry Travis. Honestly, where are we going to go now? You don't know. You don't have the faintest idea where this guy has gone. I vote we just enjoy the park until we find another clue - if we find another clue."

"Travis, Luci," Hank interrupted, always the peacemaker. "Look at the line. Everyone quit the queue 10 minutes ago, and they just opened it. It's a seven minute wait!"

"See? How often does that happen, Travis? The Fracker is calling us." Luci was insistent. "Come on, let's get in this line now."

"Ok, Ok, I'm good." Travis shrugged. He couldn't really argue with that kind of logic, the short line was a fabulous opportunity and it was true he didn't know where to go next. If they rode the Fracker, maybe he'd get another look at that circuit?

The three of them practically ran through the line again, passing all the props, only this time Hank noticed Hawaii had a few extra islands marked in purple. That was pretty funny.

"Check out Hawaii Luci." Just as she looked, another island bubbled up on the map.

"That's hilarious." Luci called back to Hank who shouted, "I think I'll call it Hankdom."

They made the flume in less than five minutes. Strapped in again, they drifted though the warehouse and bulging pipes. As they rounded the corner into the disaster room, Travis focused on the control panel, sparking ominously. For the first time, he realized the danger being represented of the electrical lines so close to the water. It was another detail he'd missed all these years. As the panel sparked he turned his attention to the floor in anticipation of the bubbling. The lights went out, the emergency lights came on, and suddenly he remembered! The workman Mike said someone had burned the box, trying to set the circuit breakers on fire! The intruder wasn't trying to get inside Mt. Alta, he was trying to stop the park.

As the flume reached the precipice, Travis glanced over towards the service path. The flume slowly eased over the edge, hovering out into open space then slowly the weight tilted it downward… and then bam! They dropped through roiling water, past heated mist and sudden geysers. His stomach dropped as they spun into a tunnel that sends them plummeting. They wound around and down a cement tube, into a metal turbine with bent blades that just barely miss them. Spinning along the cement curve through the blades, the flume flowed out of the turbine like a breath of fresh air out into the island jungle. It carried them down a smaller drop, along a refreshing stream bed, over rocks and through palms, finally ending in the paradise of a calm pool and exit docks near the 'Gad About' lazy river. Across the pool, the turbines from the Vonderheist cast moving shadows on the dock. It was industrial and natural at the same time.

"You made it! Congratulations! We were so worried." Said a voice over the intercom as staffers in fire singed lab coats helped unload the flumes. As they walked out of the exit, Travis turned to watch the empty flumes disappear into a cave to be loaded on the other side.

"I LOVE it!" Luci and Hank gave each other a high five as they walked up the dock.

"That was incredible! Did you see that turbine, I had to close my eyes; it really looked like we would hit it. I'm pretty sure it brushed my hair!"

"It didn't brush your hair Luci - that was just a little puff of wind from a fan they have." Travis laughed. He loved the Fracker. It was a lot of fun, and he'd figured something out. He wanted to tell them, but he was afraid Luci might realize she was right about riding the Fracker again, so he decided to keep that little tidbit to himself. There was plenty of time to share.

"Its 1:30 guys," Travis said. "We need to head over to the Wrennaisance Theatre for the coaster. Our appointment is at 2:00, its best to get there about 15 minutes before hand."

"And we're off." Luci added, with a big smile. The three of them marched in a loud clomping bundle of energy, headed towards Shell Plaza.

They had just passed the entrance to the Sue Namee wave pool when a glowing bit of rock on their right distracted them.

"Again?" Luci stopped and pointed at the rock. "Who is this for?"

There was no one around, it had to be them, but none of their teletabs were flashing?

"I'll take it!" They all looked over at Travis as he pulled out his teletab and started flipping through his keys.

"You got it buddy!" Hank stepped aside.

"I haven't really done anything today?" With the exception of that hack key, which still confused him, Travis hadn't gathered anything new today. He couldn't think of any new gadgets his current keys could solve.

"Don't question the gods of Mt. Alta, dude." Hank gave a little mock hang ten gesture to emphasize his point. He was punchy, obviously feeling good today about the whole toggle thing.

"No reason to look a gift portal in the mouth." Luci laughed as well; she was downright giddy over the potential for another toggle.

Travis prepared himself as he quickly thought through keys. He only had a couple of particularly strange ones - a coil, foot pedals – but he stepped into the portal. He was hesitant, but ready to take on the challenge. Luci and Hank remained outside looking in, expecting to watch Travis work the screen, but just as his keys loaded up the portal door slipped closed! Suddenly, Travis was alone, in the portal, and the darkness around him didn't make him feel any better.

"Remain calm." He told himself. "You can do this."

The screen glowed blue and Travis began manipulating his keys. He tried connecting the coil to an iron lever. "Maybe it's an electro magnet?" It didn't work. He tried moving a cog up to connect to the foot pedals. Nothing clicked together. A warning beacon began blinking to alert Travis that he was running out of time. Travis moved faster, spinning keys around, trying to find connections, trying to be inspired. The beeping grew faster as well, like a bomb. Without warning, the screen flashed, the beacon flashed red, an alarm sounded and all went dark.

For a moment Travis was just depressed that he'd failed the puzzle but the silent portal was closed tight. He waited in the dark for the door to open, but it didn't. Travis felt his way along the rock wall, trying to find a button or a lever to open the portal, but he couldn't find one. He called out to Luci and Hank but no one responded. Panicking, Travis realized he was trapped, inside the rock - in the dark. As he tried to focus in the blackness, Travis imagined he was seeing flames in the distance. He thought he could see pirates dancing below him. A terror seized him and he closed his eyes, clinging to the rock wall behind him.

15

Stuck

Outside the portal, Luci and Hank patiently waited for a minute or two, but became increasingly alarmed when it failed to open again.

"What the heck?" Hank asked as he began looking for a groove or something to pull the doors open.

"Is this normal?" Luci asked. "Is this something Travis did?"

"No, it's not normal." Hank was getting nervous. Travis didn't have enough toggles, he couldn't possibly have gained access into the cave. He tried to find the door, a seam, anything to indicate the portal existed but the rock face wouldn't budge!

"Luci, you need to go get help." Hank started to pound on the portal. He was frustrated. He hoped it might make the door open but he also wanted to communicate with Travis. He needed to let Travis know he was not alone.

"Go see if you can find someone who works here." Hank said as he pounded on the rock. Luci took one look at the panic on Hank's face and dashed off down the path.

"Travis?" Hank began yelling at the rock. "We're working on it. We're getting help. Travis if you can hear me, we're coming."

Inside the portal Travis thought he heard his name. He wanted to get up and walk to the portal door, but in the dark, it looked like an open abyss between him and the door. He could hear voices but he was frozen. Travis closed his eyes and tried to focus on the pounding. It was like a heart beat, letting him know someone was coming.

"Travis, it's OK." On the other side of the portal, Hank kept pounding and reassuring Travis help was on the way. He couldn't hear Travis but a shuffle of rocks behind him alerted Hank that Luci was back.

"I found this guy coming down the path." Luci was breathing heavy from running. "He's an engineer and he can help."

Hank looked up to see a bearded man in a light flannel shirt and dorky black shoes.

"I understand you're having a problem with the portal?"

Hank nodded. The man seemed friendly enough, even if he did dress a little old fashioned.

"Our friend is stuck in there. We need to get him out quick."

"I think I can fix that." The man went around the side of the rock.

"We're coming Travis." Hank shouted. Luci stood back watching them. Not sure what to do, she just stood at ready.

Hank was pounding on the door when abruptly, the rock shifted, and as easy as that, the portal slid opened. No lights, no fanfare, just an open portal.

Hank and Luci ran up to the door to find Travis by the blank screen. He was getting up, wiping his face and trying to look composed.

"Thanks." He mumbled sheepishly. Luci put her arm around his shoulder and Hank sort of stood there, not knowing what to say.

"Are you OK? How freaky was that!" Luci stepped back, a little embarrassed.

"Thanks for getting the door open." Travis looked at Hank grateful. "I could hear you inside."

"I wasn't sure. You didn't answer." Hank replied.

"I…" Travis hesitated, "I didn't want to use up all my oxygen." He looked at Hank and Luci to see if that satisfied their curiosity about why he didn't answer them. "Thanks for getting the door open though."

"I didn't do it." Hank explained. "Luci did, or at least Luci found this guy, who knew how to open the door. There's a panel with something like a safety switch just around the side of the rock." Hank added. "Right over there." Hank pointed to the rock.

Travis was fascinated by the portal switch concept and couldn't resist going around the rock to try and find it. They expected to find the man on the other side of the bush but he was gone!

"Where is he?" Confused, Luci turned around. "He was right here."

Hank and Luci scanned the crowd for any sign of their helper. It was weird. Luci's brain was spinning with ideas. She wondered why the portal closed in the first place. Was someone trying to stop them? And who was that guy? How did he know about the panel?

"Where did that guy go? Hank asked the obvious.

"I don't know," Luci's brow was wrinkled with worry.

"Well, you're the one who found him, how did you find him?" Hank asked.

"He was just walking down the path." Luci said. "Jogging actually. You're right. I think he knew an awful lot about that portal."

"I guess that makes sense then." Hank said.

Luci turned confused, "How does that make sense?"

"I'm guessing he was the game master. Right? I mean, he looked a little dorky you know."

"Why would the game master be hanging out next to the Fracker?"

"So, the game master walks the park." Hank added dismissively. "That's not such a stretch and it's not that scary either. The game master knows the portals and the mechanics of how to open them, so it makes sense." Hank didn't see the reason for her suspicion.

"But we were following the intruder." Travis broke his silence.

"Which means maybe, the intruder was responsible for the portal." Luci said slowly.

Travis' eyes suddenly grew big. She was right! They were chasing the intruder on Mt. Alta when the Fracker went down "Do you think as we were following him, he was following us?" He asked.

Luci looked at him suddenly horrified. It was terrifying to think that some strange man had been following them throughout the park.

"Could that guy have been the intruder?" Travis asked again.

"No. He couldn't be." Luci said confused. "He was too nice."

"Maybe, the game master was also following the intruder." Hank said.

"You know what, that could be Hank." Travis said. "It makes sense. Or maybe he just knew the portal had malfunctioned."

In any case, Travis was just glad to be out of the portal. The warm sun brightened his mood and calmed him down. The fact that they might have just met the game master cheered them up a bit and they stood, thinking in the sun for just a moment, until Travis checked the time on his teletab and suddenly realized with a sinking feeling, it was almost 2:00.

"Guys, we need to be at the Wrenaissance Theatre!"

16

The Wrenaissance Theatre of Wonders

"**W**E'RE LATE!" TRAVIS STARTED RUNNING recklessly down the path to the plaza. In seconds, he was clearing the trees and hitting the crowds with Luci and Hank close behind him. The Wrenaissance Theatre was all the way across the plaza from the Centrifuge. They could easily see the theatre, a Beaux Arts style building with elegant columns, but they still needed to go through the line. Travis, Hank and Luci ran across the plaza dodging through the crowds, trying to make it in time.

"Are you sure this is right? Luci kept turning back around to check behind them. "How do you know this is right?"

"Luci, come on!" Travis was getting more and more anxious about making the line counter. If they didn't make it by 2:00 they would have to get another appointment for his coaster design.

The queue followed a winding path past a series of sculptures, ferns and large palms. In the midst of the garden they came upon an iron garden gate made of large gears and a huge openwork timepiece. It was a clock that scanned your teletab and allowed you into the gate – if you were on time!

Travis, Luci and Hank slipped past the clock in the nick of time. It was exactly 1:59 and just after they passed, the clock began chiming.

"We made it!" Travis made a visible sigh of relief and they stopped to catch their breath.

"Are you trying to kill us?" Hank was tanked and Luci joined him on a bench just around the corner. Palms, bromeliads and flowering orchids decorated a shady niche and marble statues of philosophers, dignitaries and Saints lined the garden walls.

Hank stopped huffing briefly to point out one of the carvings, "Check out the head he's holding - it's the headless horseman!"

"No, its not, it's Saint Denis." Luci corrected him. "He's a Christian Saint, beheaded on Montmarte in Paris. According to legend he picked up his head and walked six miles, preaching the whole time. He's the patron saint against frenzy and strife. Which is kinda' funny when you think about it." And she looked pointedly at Travis.

"How do you know this stuff?" Hank was often amazed by Luci's endless knowledge of what seem like random facts.

"I read. This guy sort of stands out you know - with the head and all."

"Yes he does." Hank said, standing back up. "OK. I'm ready."

Back on the move, they passed a shaded pond, where two large birds, pink like flamingos, but with wide bills like a duck, were in the water. Luci recognized them first.

"Check out the spoonbills! They're eating….look!"

Luci was impressed; she'd never seen a real Roseate spoonbill before. She snapped a quick picture for her gallery. Travis looked with her and paused.

"That's weird." He said. He didn't remember animals being on Hoverpark before. It was a good idea.

Heavy marble columns framed an open porch and the stairs led up to a large wooden door. As they walked through the open gates toward the doorway, loud voices from behind them suddenly interrupted their progress.

"Travis!" Travis, Hank and Luci turned around to see their classmates - Madison, Sean, and Sidney - running up to them.

"What's up guys?" Madison said. She was sweet on Travis. Travis barely noticed her but Hank couldn't help thinking that Madison had very pretty hair. It was shiny brown, with blond highlights and she wore it in a little sassy ponytail that she flipped around like a fishing lure.

"We saw you talking to One - Eyed Cy earlier." Madison tried to get Travis' attention.

Hank took the bait. "Yeah, we saw this strange man and..." He started to share their adventures, but stopped abruptly as Luci literally punched his shoulder. "Cy is pretty creepy. He totally got us in trouble with Ms. Edison."

"Ms. Edison is such a nudge. She's always on your back." Madison glanced at Travis to see if he caught her vote of sympathy.

"What have you done so far?" Sean stepped up to save them all from Madison.

"We've been on the Centrifuge, the Vonderheist and the Fracker." Luci, Hank and Travis compared notes on their morning.

"Sheesh - How did you get all that done? We waited forever in line for the Fracker. It took up most of our morning."

"We got lucky. The line went down when they closed the ride for a little bit this morning."

"And Travis has been running us ragged." Hank was still breathing a little heavy. "He designed a coaster special - want to join us?" Hank invited them, much to Luci's chagrin.

"Sure - Syd, is that OK with you?" Sean turned to Sydney who nodded smiling.

"That sounds super'licious!" Madison added. "It's a date."

Luci rolled her eyes and wondered again what Sydney saw in Madison.

Together, they entered the large hall which was lined with oversized gold framed mirrors, marble sideboards and velvet couches. A glass case contained several photos of dirigibles - some featuring a smiling Dr. Wren - and a trophy flanked by elaborate blue ribbons. Everything implied a bold opening for the MEEAD Center's latest technological advances. Stray champagne glasses were scattered about as if a party was in progress. Shadows in bowler caps, and elegant skirts intermingled on the other side of closed glass doors. The sound of violins and laughter echoed through the lines.

Luci paused to admire a framed bit of Victorian lace and flowers, shaped like a heart and surrounding the name 'Ada' written in calligraphy. It resembled art she'd once seen in a history museum, but something about it seemed familiar. Who was Ada?

"I know this one," Luci said to herself. "It's going to drive me nuts."

"Ada Lovelace" Sydney said quietly as she stood beside Luci.

"Of course!" Luci was surprised and pleased. "She invented computer coding." Luci always did like Sydney, even if they weren't the best of friends. Sydney smiled and nodded and Luci decided she should probably get to know her better.

"Quick, they're leaving us behind." Luci said. She and Sydney ran to catch up to the rest of the group.

As they reached a grand staircase, a tux wearing young gentleman accepted guest's 'tickets' and directed them to the appropriate doorway. There were approximately twelve simulators on two floors running concurrently. You could chose quick custom design, with features added in line terminals or you could load a ride of your own design like Travis. As Travis, Luci and Hank came through the line, the butler directed them into a private waiting room.

"How many in your party, Sir?" He asked.

"We've got six." Luci answered. Hank laughed.

"Room 10 upstairs." The butler responded, directing them to the carpeted ramp with an open gloved hand. A large bird of paradise was growing in the glassed atrium, surrounded by other tropical plants.

"Your public awaits you." He said.

They filed up the ramp, their voices echoing in the great hall below as they passed the crystal chandelier hanging from the glass ceiling. "Your public awaits you" Hank laughed, mocking the butler's parting phrase. He had to admit though, it was pretty glorious. Travis was sharing his test ride with a small group of friends, but the ride would be available for the rest of the day as well, so they could tell their classmates and connect them to it directly. It was Travis' instant fifteen minutes of fame.

The entrance to Room 10 led them into a waiting room where an antique looking screen flashed the coaster schematic. Here they could make a few canned adjustments to their ride. There were actually options for parkers to add to the Hoverpark's existing coasters. It was 'decorate your own cupcake' design and Travis wasn't too keen on these alterations to his masterpiece, but since everyone was having so much fun, it didn't seem right to protest.

Luci stepped up to the board and added a hoard of locusts in the first dip, Sydney added frogs in the second dip and spitting vipers on the third curve and Sean adjusted the initial drop to include a thunderstorm. "Mood enhancers' they called it, though Travis was not very impressed.

"Relax Travis," Hank nudged his friend. "I have a good feeling about this."

Two large doors opened with a flourish into a low lit, windowless room. The walls were covered in thick red drapes. Another staffer, this time a 'French maid,' directed them to the only furniture in the room; a very rusted looking metal contraption, riveted together, and perched on a series of gears and pinions. The front windshield of the rickety car glowed slightly like a computer screen.

"Good afternoon, Ladies and Gentlemen. We are pleased you could join us today and I anticipate a strong response to your ingenious invention. Be sure to secure any loose items in the lockers by the door. Your test drive will begin shortly, so please be seated. The safety bar will lower to secure you into the vehicle. For your safety we request that you attach your 6 point safety belt snugly and pull on the red flap to insure it is buckled."

"Please sir, your red flap." The French maid interrupted Sean who was still talking to Sydney and didn't hear the instructions.

"Sir, please pull on your red flap." She said again.

Sean pulled, turning a bit red himself, as everyone turned to watch. The French maid thanked him and shut the door.

"Thank you. Have a safe journey. Your experiment will begin shortly!" She said.

As the room went dark, the vehicle's screen came on and the simulator slowly lifted. With sparks and flashes the room slowly began to glow. The curtains lifted to reveal a 360 degree panoramic vision of Travis's coaster in a surround sound studio. As a guitar solo began a slow crescendo, the vehicle started to 'climb' the track and the false screen on the car collapsed quietly, clearing the view. Enthralled, they looked around themselves excitedly on the ascent. The graphics were phenomenal; they were climbing an old wooden rollercoaster over an urban wasteland. Luci reached her hand out into the emptiness, and touched a computer generated 'tree branch' which responded!

A river beneath them wound through rapids and industrial brick warehouses. It flowed under a collapsed cement bridge and torn railroad tracks. A destroyed turbine, overgrown with vegetation gushed water back into the river. As they climbed above the roofline, they passed an old radio tower and a crumbled sign, flaking paint where once bright red letters advertised the radio station. In the distance was an old graveyard, the dead overlooking the river. The music accelerated and suddenly, dark clouds overtook the vehicle, a low rumbling began in the room, dark streaks of rain began pounding on the hood and lightning struck the tower. All the girls and Hank screamed just as the car dove down the first drop.

The car's speed blurred the scenery as they dove through the ironworks, chimneys blasting all around them. The heat radiated off the machinery - gears and pistons pumping - and they crashed through a warehouse towards the river. Suddenly there were grasshoppers everywhere, a regular plague leaping out of the trees and bushes, but the car moved up out of the grasshoppers only to slip into the darkness of a brick warehouse. The smell of heat, tobacco and hot wind swept past them, sparks flying, as the coaster climbed, through wooden doors and iron scaffolding then out onto the roof. Another breathtaking view of the skyline, this time in the dark, and all around them comets swept past and crashed on the ground.

It was an asteroid shower of explosive proportions! With a sudden twist and drop, the car looped upside down and around in a corkscrew to avoid a large comet. Then, it dipped back down into darkness, branches and the sound of rushing water combines with the slimy flopping of leaping frogs. One squish hit Luci's face which was disgusting! She heard Madison scream however and wasn't too upset.

The car rolled out around the curve and headed into a large curving dip over the river then slam, they lost power dropping rapidly into the water! Rushing rapids roiled past them, and the car acted as if it would spin out of control. Water was splashing into the car and everyone shrieked with laughter as they teetered alongside a rock bank. They were hooting with joy as the car spun over a canal lock, under a bridge and then up above the tree line again looping over the cemetery. They passed - in no particular order - mausoleums, large ornate angels, a rock pyramid monument, crosses and towers spinning in large loops. Then, just as they dove for another drop, leaping vipers jumped out of the branches! The car swept under them, snake venom splashed, but the car wound around the railroad track and past the water tower. After two more curves through industrial welding shops with sparks flying, they slipped into the station at the end of the track.

The song ended, the room went dark and as the simulator docked lighting returned to reveal the curtained screens again. Their seatbelts clicked open. In less than 7 minutes the ride was over. A loud clapping from the speakers accompanied their own cheers, with interspersed bouts of 'Bravo' and 'Good Show'.

"Awesome Travis!" The whole group resounded with praise for Travis' coaster. Hank and Sean offered 'high fives' and Madison beamed with pride.

"What a blast!" Luci said, ignoring Madison's preening as they dug their purses out of the lockers.

"Those frogs were a nice touch!" Luci glanced over at Sydney who grinned back at her.

"Gross." Madison practically slapped her for mentioning them. "Both of you. Just gross."

Sydney coughed nervously. Luci wasn't sure, but she thought Sydney might be laughing.

17

Surprises

THEY LEFT ROOM 10 IN a chattering cluster, following the exit signs. As they started down a carpeted ramp, a new butler approached Travis with an old handset phone on a tray, elegantly covered with a linen cloth. "Excuse me sir, there's a phone call for you." He handed Travis the handset. Hesitant, Travis put the phone carefully to his ear - he'd never used a phone like that before and wasn't sure what to expect. To his relief, a loud voice boomed over the earpiece.

"Fine job, young man! If you'll please join me in the library, I've arranged for a small token of my appreciation for your accomplishment!"

Travis stood puzzled with his friends around him. The butler swept his hand towards a side door and everyone joined him inside. The room was filled with books, floor to ceiling and there was a ladder to reach the higher ones. An unusually tall writing desk was located just to the left of a raven in a cage. In the center of the room, a leather wingback chair slowly spun around as they entered. They hesitated slightly, expecting an animatronics version of Dr. Wren. Instead of a person, however it was a printer… creating a toggle!

Madison gazed all googly eyed at Travis. "That is so cool!"

"I thought you had to put together a puzzle to get a toggle?" Luci was confused.

"Me too," Travis glowed. "I don't know what happened. Maybe the coaster was a puzzle?"

"It's not very consistent. Is it?" Luci had a tendency to question a lot.

"No. It's not, not today at least." Travis admitted. It was a bit unusual. But the game master made the rules and perhaps this was an advanced toggle? Or maybe this was part of the coaster design program he'd hacked into? It was his sixth toggle however. One more to go!

Travis wore his new toggle with pride as they stepped out into the sunlit atrium. The high ceilings echoed with his friend's voices. It was the first time he'd received a toggle with an audience of his friends and Travis fairly beamed with pride. His glory was short lived however.

The once composed and elegant hall had erupted into a flurry of panicking 'butlers' and 'maids.' They had been forgotten.

Standing in the hallway, they overheard several staffers on their radios.

"I can't get the doors open"

"Turn it off then!"

"I can't. It should turn off, but something is wrong. We hit the emergency button, but it only stops the car, not the screens."

A control panel in the wall was open and a group of staffers were gathered around it arguing.

"I did that already, it won't turn off. The panel isn't responding at all."

"What about a manual override? We can shut everything down by hand."

"I'm telling you, the panel won't respond at all."

"Can't you override it?"

"I need an override code. We alerted operations and they are trying to find the manager who will have the code…then I can try again."

"It has been almost three minutes! Can't someone do something?"

Three minutes didn't seem that long, but when those minutes are in an off tilt simulator…even the most die-hard coaster fan might get a bit queasy! To make matters worse, the line to get in was growing out of control. At the front door of the theatre, the line was trailing into the garden. A butler sent to the front to control the crowd was gently correcting a particularly unruly parker. A woman in a poof hairdo kept trying to march past the line to make demands at the front. The butler stepped into her path.

"Excuse me Ma'am, we are having some technical difficulties. Please remain in line. I assure you your public awaits and your presentation will begin shortly."

The poodle woman stepped back in a huff, only to stir up more trouble in the line. Travis, Luci, Hank and their friends watched as again the butler was called upon to correct another 'break away' trying to get on the broken attraction. Luci chuckled to herself, wishing Mrs. Poof was stuck in a car in an endless freefall. Behind them they could hear alarms going off from the ride safety sensors, and a canned voice kept repeating, "For your safety, please remain seated."

A manager was talking over the soundtrack on the loudspeaker, "Please remain seated. We are experiencing brief technical difficulties and are doing what we can to complete your experiment."

Over the manager's voice, in the background you could hear someone shouting, "They're throwing up in rooms 2 and 4 as well. Someone has to stop this." and the speaker suddenly went mute.

"Jeez Louise, I'm glad we're off already!" the normally quiet Sydney chimed in on the chaos.

"No kidding," Travis added and looked knowingly at Luci and Hank.

They stood around in a bit of a shock, watching the commotion in the hall. Even Travis was confused about what to do next. Finally, a security guard grabbed their attention and swept the whole lot of them to an emergency exit.

"Follow that path to the gate. It will take you out to the main plaza." he said, adding "Consider yourself lucky and find a place to relax for bit."

Travis led them down the path, which was thankfully quiet enough for them to talk.

"What do you think, Travis?" Luci asked quietly. She was walking in front of the group alongside Travis and the others were excitedly chatting behind them.

"I'm not sure what is going on." Travis answered. "On dark rides, the scenes run even when the cars are stopped. I'm surprised these cars are set up the same way? It doesn't really make sense."

"Maybe they aren't set up that way?" Luci said thoughtfully. "The staff seemed really stressed out, like more so than usual."

Travis got very quiet. Luci usually read people very well. And she was right - there was a lot more confusion than you'd expect. Even in the security fuss earlier this morning with Tara and Travis's Mom, all the staffers had really been quite calm. Travis and Luci gave each other the 'eye' but they didn't want to clue their classmates in on it, so they walked along the path under the trees, waiting for a moment when they could talk alone. Hank was hanging back with the others, enjoying the chatter and Madison's perfume. In a bold gesture, Madison suddenly dashed up front, between Luci and Travis and grabbed Travis' arm.

Madison was marching along clinging boldly to Travis. Her pony tail bounced from side to side as she pranced. Travis wistfully tossed Luci the 'help' look as Madison choked up on Travis' arm. She actually turned around slightly to give Luci a self-satisfied little smile!

"Hmmfff" Luci couldn't stand it. Madison was a walking poster child of ignorance and small minded pettiness. Luci didn't play those games normally, but since the gloves had been tossed, she decided to rise to the occasion! Shoulders back, head up, Luci shifted into 'fists for hands' mode and took aim. Sensing the sparks, Hank wisely shoved himself between Luci and Madison, blocking the shot. He then pushed through Travis and Madison and marched toward the gate.

On the other side of the gate, they turned the corner around a large tree to find themselves out in the bright sun. They were at the edge of the main plaza close to the train tracks. Everyone around them seemed to be in a bad mood. The train's steam whistle echoed across the park and they looked up to see an extra large group of people on the sail train. Some of the people were even clinging to the boarding rails. No one was smiling and that struck Luci as a bit odd. It was not near as strange however as the scene across the Plaza. The Centrifuge was a quarter of the way up but completely still. A female voice over the loud speaker interrupted the usual soundtrack.

"Attention all guests; we are experiencing a temporary interruption in service. We apologize for any inconvenience. If you are currently on a stalled attraction, please remain seated- someone will assist you shortly."

The chaos had Luci on edge. Travis was noticeably tense as well. What were they going to do if the park was under attack?

"Well, I'm ready for an ice cream float or a Marvy soda." Madison lilted at the general group. "Who's with me?"

"What a total idiot." Luci mumbled. She couldn't restrain herself.

"What?" Madison glanced over at Luci like a cricket had chirped.

"I'm in. Syd and I are parched, aren't you Syd?" Sean spoke up quickly. Sydney nodded as well.

"Travis?" Madison batted her eyes over at Travis.

"Naw, you guys go on. We'll see you later." Travis took the opening to get away and waved goodbye with a genuine smile. Madison was mortified, but smiled back at her friends and sashayed across the plaza toward the grab truck.

"Thanks again Trav." Sean turned to say goodbye. "That was really great!" Sydney nodded and they ran after Madison.

18

Trouble in Paradise

Visibly relieved Madison was gone, Travis turned to face Luci and Hank. They were obviously hot, Hank was sweating badly actually, and Luci looked tired, her eyes were glazed a bit in the bright sun. Travis was feeling the heat as well, but he tended to plow through his exhaustion with full force action and adrenaline.

"Well, it looks like our intruder has definitely been busy" He stated emphatically, looking at both of them. "I have a theory…" Travis began.

"A theory?" Hank practically wilted. "The whole idea that there even is an intruder is a theory."

"What do you mean?" Travis came back at him. "You saw the intruder too?"

"I saw someone working on a breaker box." Hank corrected him. "For all you know, it was a maintenance guy for the Hoverpark, or it could have been…." Hank was afraid to say 'ghost', "It could have just been an engineer working on a routine electrical problem?" Hank was getting tired of all the drama. "Honestly," he thought to himself, "why does everything have to be so earth shattering? Maybe there is just some electrical stuff going on? Maybe it is a good time for a snack. And just maybe it would have been fun to go with Madison, Sydney and Sean?"

"By 'routine electrical problems' you mean the fire someone started under circuit breaker box by the Hydro-dam?" Travis lost his temper. "You don't know the first thing about it, Hank. I was the one brave enough to go. You just sat in the flume. And there is no such thing as a routine fire Hank. Just how do you think a fire on the outside of a circuit breaker box gets started? Are you proposing spontaneous combustion?"

Travis pounded Hank with questions. He knew he was right. The intruder had set fire to the breaker to try and stop the park. And the intruder was still trying to stop the park. He just knew this was why the park was so wonky. And Hank was supposed to support him. What kind of a friend was he? Travis was mad and his words were bitter and angry.

"Well?" He asked again vehemently, oozing in sarcasm.

Hank's face scrunched up in anger and shock. He wasn't used to Travis being so brutal. Neither he nor Luci expected such nastiness from Travis. Hank was stunned and silent, but Luci wasn't. She was used to bullies and she wasn't one to shy away from berating outbursts. Without hesitating, Luci turned and faced Travis with some choice words of her own.

"Who do you think you are Travis? You can't talk to Hank that way. He's been following you around all day, doing what you want to do. He's allowed to have his own opinion. You're just being a jerk. And you've basically been lying to us. You never said a word about a fire. When did you learn about this fire? What else have you been lying about?"

"I just forgot about the fire." Travis lied quietly. "But we need to do something. I think the intruder is trying to shut down the park. Or destroy it even, did you ever think of that? What about all these people here? What about us for that matter? What are we going to do? We are the only ones that can stop it."

"What are you talking about Travis? Have you gone bonkers? You have no power to stop this, so don't even go there. You don't know where the intruder is or what he is doing. None of us do. We have to wait, just like everyone else. Furthermore, if we had gone looking for the intruder, you wouldn't have gotten to ride the coaster you designed and you wouldn't have gotten your new toggle."

Luci had lost her patience with Travis' moping. Travis and Hank were both rather floored at the speed with which she jumped down Travis' throat. It distracted Hank somewhat and embarrassed Travis, which was the point.

Luci stared at them, noticed their large eyes and immediately regretted her outburst. Their open silent faces brought a calming guilt. Almost apologetically, Luci added, "Sometimes, you just have to wait for villains to make their next move. There is nothing you can do about it and there's no use banging your head against a rock. Keep your sanity, and your good humor. You need a strong spirit to fight a creep like this guy."

The three of them stood there quietly for a minute, Hank shuffling his feet, Luci waiting for Travis to say something and Travis - well, Travis was sometimes a bit slow on apologies. If he was at fault, he tended to focus on a diversion. Mentally, he just didn't quite get the apology business.

"OK, so I did forget about the fire, but don't you see how important it is?" Travis looked around to see if the new story had hooked them. One glance at their faces however and Travis realized, even his brilliant intruder theory couldn't distract them from his rude outburst. But it was important! He knew he was wrong, but can't we just move on? The theory was so much more interesting.

Travis tried again, "Don't you get it? I think the whole park is in trouble now. I think the intruder has taken over the park!" He said.

Luci gave Travis a long stare. Hank kept looking at his shoes and taking tentative glances at Luci and Travis. In silence, Luci's stare became more and more uncomfortable until finally Travis took the less than subtle hint.

"OK. You're right. I'm sorry, I was a jerk. Seriously, I am sorry." Travis said begrudgingly.

Luci continued to look silently at him. Hank, still wounded, glanced up wanting to forget, but Luci was still oozing with the spikes of her hot temper. Hank knew better than to offend Luci when she was in this mood. And honestly, she was in the right. She was defending him even. Hank looked back down at his shoes and shuffled.

"What do you want? I'm sorry." Travis tried to find a peace offering, "Ok, how about I buy you both a 'Marvy soda'? Will that help?"

"It might." Luci sniffed. Hank smiled. He was actually ok with 'sorry' but he figured a Marvy wouldn't hurt.

"Then will you listen to my theory? I'm serious. I think we might be in trouble." Travis was grateful to get past this and ready to move on.

"I'm game." Hank said smiling. He was secretly pleased that Luci has stepped up to support him. He appreciated it. But now she was being a bit dramatic.

Still fuming, Luci followed them both to Ma Ridgley's Courtyard. Hank gave her a little shoulder hug to thank her for defending him - and to encourage her to drop the attitude.

They stopped off at a grab truck that was still operating even through the brown out. The cart sold ice cold Marvys, some snack packs and a selection of small cog-shaped bundt cakes. Hank got a frosted strawberry coglet to share. Together they found a seat in the gardens, tucked away from the masses of people. Quietly they sat, sipping on their sodas and watching the crowd. It was meltdown city, children were crying, adults showed their ugly nature and generally everyone needed to calm down.

Travis and Hank started mocking one young couple struggling with three kids dressed to the nines in goggles and hats, all of them insisting on different things to do, all of them insisting they weren't loved, while hugging toys, and purchased keys, Marvys and cog cakes. It was pretty funny. Rich parkers lived a bit differently than local kids. It was nice to know they weren't particularly happier for it.

Luci sipped her soda silently at first, and listened to the boys. Their laughter was infectious and slowly, she perked up. Luci was never one to actually hold a grudge. Not for too long at least. It just took her a little to calm down again after she got mad.

Once they finished their sodas, and relaxed a while in the shade Travis tried again. He could hardly control his excitement, and he wanted more than anything to share this new theory with his friends.

"I've been thinking about everything that's happened since we've been here. First there was the incident with Tara at the entrance. Luci, you saw that there was another intruder, someone other than the woman they arrested." Travis said.

Luci nodded and Travis continued, "Then there was the fire by the Fracker, remember how the Fracker stopped right at that time? I'm thinking that fire was set by our intruder. And we just saw what's going on in the Wrenaissance Theatre. I think it's all connected. I think the intruder is doing these things, sabotaging the whole park."

"But why?" Luci asked. "What is the purpose?"

"I'm not sure of that. But don't forget the portal; you know we didn't get much of a chance to talk about me getting caught in that portal? What if he was responsible for the portal too?"

"Why would he trap you in a portal Travis?" Luci was found of conspiracy theories, but she preferred to take rational leaps of faith. "What would he gain by doing that?"

"Maybe he knows we're looking for him? Maybe he's trying to stop us." Travis began.

"Maybe," Luci pondered that for a moment. "He'd be pretty stupid not to notice we've been following him around."

"But to him we're just a bunch of kids Luci." Hank offered his rare analysis. "No one pays much attention to kids. Not usually anyway."

Luci and Travis nodded.

"That's true." Travis said. It was worth thinking about, even if it was just for the sake of an adventure.

In silence they all sipped on their Marvys watching parkers run around confused. A voice came over the speakers again,

"Attention all guests; we are currently experiencing a temporary interruption in service. We apologize for any inconvenience. If you are currently on a stalled attraction, please remain seated - someone will assist you shortly."

"They said the same thing fifteen minutes ago. Those rides aren't going to be running for a while. It'll be forever before they get the guests off the current rides. Imagine what you would do on the GENsys? There must be at least 100 people suspended on the chair lifts inside the planetarium." Travis was rambling on about the evacuation process when Luci suddenly interrupted him.

"Travis! What time did your Mom say she was meeting Tara and her friends at the GENsys?" Luci asked.

"2:30, Why? Oh, crap." Travis realized it was highly possible they were stuck on the GENsys! He was now much more invested in the evacuation. "We've got to get over there."

19

The GENsys

THE GENsys WAS IN BEE Plaza, across from Amy's Conservatory and the hanging gardens, which meant they had to go through Ma Ridgely's - again. It was particularly crowded. The traffic was increasing dramatically by the minute and based on the ice cream and snack carts being rolled into the plazas, this was a trend that park management had noticed. Everyone was taking a break and trying to get lunch. Kids were climbing on the water fountains. Lines were long, people were hoarding seats at the tables, and everywhere tensions rose.

Travis, Luci and Hank had to walk through this wriggling soup and fast.

"Try to find a path through family groups" Travis yelled back at Luci and Hank, as he dashed behind a stroller, weaving into the crowd at an angle. He almost slammed into a young couple that came to a dead stop right in front of him. The woman pulled out her telctab and pointed something out to her companion. Why can't people just pull over to the side to look at a map!

"We're behind you Travis, just keep going!" Luci and Hank were slower but following Travis' red mop of hair through the crowd. Once in the plaza, they had walk against traffic to get back out through the wall of people coming directly at them. Travis moved to the far right along the brickwork and headed into the hanging gardens at the conservatory. Directly across from them, through the sea of people, was the GENsys.

Travis hesitated. He could stop but he turned and called back to Hank and Luci, "I can't wait. Meet me there! Do what you can." He jumped into the fray of people going absolutely perpendicular to the flow of traffic. Luci and Hank tried to follow but it was hard. They could barely make out Travis in the masses, but then Hank saw him rise up to shoulder height and dash along a garden wall. Luci looked up to sight him in, just as he leapt into the crowd a good 50 yards ahead of them. Obviously, the stress had made Travis a bit nervy.

"Ummph!" Luci was smacked in the calf by a stroller carrying a sleeping infant. She turned to face the stroller driver, a bitter looking woman with blond hair plastered into elegant curls on top of her head. The lady pulled the stroller back and rammed it into her again.

"Hey!" Luci exclaimed.

"Excuse me." The woman said, "I'm trying to go through here."

"You can wait! That stroller isn't a battering ram. What is wrong with you?" Luci started.

The stroller lady shrugged ambivalently, and Luci stopped walking and slowly turned around like a dueling gunslinger. Hank stepped in just then, placing his hand on her shoulder and with a nod reminded Luci that Travis was on the move.

"Watch it lady." Luci remarked as she dove back into the crowd. Hank grinned - just a little.

As they popped out of the mass of parkers, Luci and Hank saw Travis dashing up the entrance to the GENsys. The entrance was obviously closed but at the other side of the building, at the gift shop, was the exit. Travis leapt over the hedge and ran into the gift shop. By the slow trickle of guests wandering out the door, it seemed there was a complicated evacuation in progress. Travis ran up to the first available staff member who was wearing an elaborately decorated white tunic.

"Sir, I'm pretty sure my family is on the GENsys." Travis asked.

"We are currently evacuating the GENsys," the staffer explained while directing other guests to continue past the attraction. "Move along folks, service at the GENsys has been interrupted. Please return a little later."

Travis remained looking alarmingly at a note from his Mom on his teletab.

"Mom and Tara are in there, stuck." He said to Luci and Hank. Travis was talking at the teletab, "We're out here Mom, and we're on our way."

"Travis honey," the voice of Mrs. Pruitt could be heard over Travis' teletab, "They are evacuating us. If you just stay put, we'll be down shortly."

Travis held his ground in front of the staffer who looked up, almost surprised to see Travis still standing there and paused to explain candidly, "Don't worry. Everything is going well. They will out anytime soon. If you'd like, you can wait over there by the benches. Everyone is being evacuated through these doors."

Travis stood there in an uncomfortable pause. He considered rushing the doors, until Luci took him firmly by the shoulder and led him toward the benches.

"Let's sit down Travis. And wait for a little while." Luci tried to be reassuring. "They'll be out soon." She glanced over at Hank, nudging him to back her up.

"Yeah, Travis," Hank offered, "Your Mom is really smart. I'm sure they're OK."

Travis was silent, breathing just a little bit shallow. He started thinking about the intruder. What was he trying to do? Why was he stopping all the attractions?

"They're probably already on their way out. It won't hurt to wait a bit." Hank added.

He was wrong, Travis thought as he stiffly sat down. It hurt. It hurt a lot.

"Travis," Luci recognized he was panicking. "It's just a theory. We don't know the intruder is trying to harm the park or any of us on it. No one has been hurt. We're all fine."

Travis nodded. They sat in silence for what seemed like forever but it was only a minute. Finally Luci pulled out her teletab.

"Look, let's work on our galleries." It was supposed to seem like a random distraction, but she didn't fool anyone. Luci had an overachieving bug like you wouldn't believe. She was already taking notes on her tagged items.

"I've got two themes really - green energy and wildlife!" Luci didn't look up. "What have you been collecting?"

Reluctantly, Hank and Travis pulled out their teletabs. Hank poked a little at his gallery but Travis only opened his for effect.

"See," Luci continued talking, "I'm thinking there might be a connection somewhere? My gallery has a lot of cycles: I have energy from photosynthesis and solar power, water filtering and plant oxygenation; somehow the wildlife must be part of a cycle?

Travis was looking down at his teletab, flipping through randomly, until he realized what Luci was saying.

"What wildlife Luci?" Travis knew better. There was no wildlife on Hoverpark. It was entirely man made.

"I've got wildlife." Hank produced a photo of a skeletal mammoth grouper from the bone room.

"That's not wildlife Hank. The optimal word here is 'life' and those are just bones." Travis said.

"Here," Luci opened up a photo of the roseate spoonbills. "This wildlife."

Travis looked at the spoonbills, remembering them and thought hard. "That's really strange Luci. Zoom in on his leg right there - see that metal ring? That bird has been tagged by someone. Why are there tagged birds on the park?"

Travis starred at the photo but it started to flash and zipped shut all of a sudden.

"Why did you do that?" He asked Luci. "I was looking at it."

"No! Now look what you've done!" Luci complained, she was starting to panic.

"Me? I didn't do anything. It's your teletab Luci, it's not working properly."

"Mine isn't either." Hank added as Travis looked down at his teletab in frustration.

"I think they are all messed up right now." Luci realized.

They glanced over at the rest of the parkers crowded around in the plaza and noticed it wasn't just them. Everyone seemed to be shaking their teletabs and yelling at each other. Blame was flying like a swarm of love bugs! It was total chaos.

With a bit of a crackle, like the shifting of a microphone, the music suddenly changed. Instead of the earthy world beat tunes typical of Bee Plaza, loud, raucous, classic rock music blasted throughout the gardens adding to the general noise and confusion. Fountains along the path to the GENsys, which normally bubbled gently to the music, became out of control geysers. Some of the guests walking by embraced the driving beat, but most of them were visibly stressed. It could be a prank, but Travis just knew it was the intruder.

To make matters worse, teletabs began giving guests random alerts and the map function quit working altogether. People were so used to the maps, they couldn't figure out how to get from one end of the park to the other without them. Guests were clumped together in groups arguing in a mass of flailing arms pointing this way, that direction, anywhere but where they were. It would have been funny if Travis hadn't looked at Luci and seen the fear in her eyes. She'd made a connection. Travis didn't want to know but he couldn't ignore it.

"What? What Luci? Out with it." Travis practically yelled.

"It's the communication system Travis. All communications are down." He knew what that meant. And a hot fear gripped Travis, deep in the pit of his stomach. Tara and his Mom were still on the GENsys. Travis needed to get inside and get them out now.

"When I say go, let's head inside." Travis was eyeing the two staffers inside the building monitoring the exit gate. They were arguing and pointing to the door and a screen in front of them. People were putting their teletabs away.

Suddenly there was a loud 'boom' as a puff of smoke blew out of the volcano. That was it - the distraction he needed. Travis jumped up just as several staffers came running out the exit doors. At least one was obviously a technical guy with his tool belt still strapped on. A security guard with them took off in the direction of the conservatory. In the chaos, Travis, Hank and Luci made their move.

"Now" Travis shouted and Luci and Hank joined him in a mad dash inside the building.

They ran through the lit hall, making the theatre in seconds flat. Inside, the room was massive, and still in semi-darkness. All around the rotunda, against the wall were columns, like teeth for the mouth of the open dome. The room was an IMAX theatre, with a center seating tower. On a good day, guests are carefully strapped in to their seats and lifted off the ground and up into the dome. The mechanics resemble a rack of seats blooming into the dome. Each seat becomes its own lifted chair that leans, tilts, and responds to the movie.

The movie itself was genuine footage of the universe in a storied trip of wonder and adventure. Parkers are cast out into the Universe during 'lift off' and they must 'find' their way home in a journey that takes them past galaxies, both Virgo and Ursa

Major, through the large and small Magellanic clouds and into the Milky Way finally finding Earth.

A portion of the movie was running on a loop. Travis recognized it. In the ride, shortly after you experience the birth of a star, you are hit by an asteroid which knocks out your computer system. Forced to navigate in manual mode, you find yourself thrown into a solar storm. It seemed the GENsys was stuck on the solar storm, a fairly sickening and disorienting segment of the movie that was tough to handle in small bouts, much less eternally looped. Even as he ran inside the dome, Travis couldn't help but wonder why it seemed the entire park was in a mixed state of limbo. It appeared the mechanics were stopped but the entertainment media was still running? It didn't matter, he had to do something. Without thinking, Travis headed towards the safety barrier that blocked the center of the room.

Gravity

In a grand leap, Travis jumped over the barrier into the ride floor and was slightly surprised an alarm did not go off. He was on the floor where the seats dock. The center was a tower of mechanical gears and arms to run the seats. He noticed the floor was scored in regular concentric circles that glowed slightly in the dark. Numbered marks on the circles, helped identify the seats when they were docked on the floor. Travis ran directly towards the center of the room.

"Mom! Tara!" Travis began shouting from the floor, near the base of the carriage.

"Here Travis, We're up here!" Mrs. Pruitt was shouting down at him.

With a heart crushing glance, Travis could see Penelope Pruitt and Tara were in the top tier, closest to the ceiling. That figured. The top tier was the most dramatic. You were immersed in the experience by the screens all around you and a virtually unobstructed view of the screens above you as well. The Pruitts loved it, and Tara and his Mom were experts at maneuvering their way into the top tier. Often, families in line would surrender their top tier spot for a calmer experience on a lower level seat. It also helped if you knew the ride well like the Pruitts. Tara would count the guests as they filed into the attraction and let people in front of her to insure her prime position. That knowledge created a real mess today however. It would take them forever to evacuate the top tier; unless, of course, they started at the top!

"We're coming to get you. Sit tight, OK" Travis yelled back up and then ran back over to Hank and Luci who were following him, somewhat slower, on the floor.

"Hank, Luci - do you see a fire?" Travis whispered. He was visibly nervous about more than the evacuation.

"No, Travis, it looks OK." Luci answered.

Travis was moving quickly, accessing the available tools and trying to figure out how the GENsys was normally evacuated. From the center of the room, he, Hank and Luci fanned out under the suspended legs. People in the chairs above them started calling down.

"Over here! They just left us…" A couple shouted over at them. The whole column of seats started talking, with each individual shouting at them.

"We need to get down as soon as possible; my daughter is waiting for us!"

"My girlfriend is panicking - can you help us get out of here?"

Travis was walking past the circles on the floor and exploring the center tower, the GENsys chassis. A barrier guarded the mechanics that lifted the chairs. Along the side of the tower was an access ladder for maintenance purposes. He had an idea.

"Hank! I need your help." Hank was still standing at the other side of the barrier. "Hank! Come on!!!"

"Honestly, Travis, I'm a bit of a GENsissy. This whole 'feet off the ground being flung through the universe' thing gives me the heebie jeebies." Hank said sheepishly.

"Well then you're really going to enjoy climbing this thing with me."

"Travis, I can't." Hank began. What was Travis thinking? The ladder was too dangerous!

"Hank, I need you. My Mom and Tara are up there and I'm going up." Travis had already started climbing up the ladder. Reluctantly, Hank climbed over the barrier and moved towards the ladder Travis was climbing. Watching Travis go up, it occurred to him, scared or not, that the mechanics of it just wasn't going to work.

"It's not going to help Travis, you can't reach them from the center." Hank shouted up at him. "Travis get down. You're not helping!"

Travis had reached the levers for the arms holding the second tier of chairs by this time. The whole thing was interlocked like giant clockworks. Travis looked out over the mechanical arms, glanced down and paused. With some reluctance he stopped what he was doing. Hank was right.

"OK." Travis called back down to Hank.

Travis was not thinking straight. The ladder would only get him up to the arms and levers, not to the chairs. He began coming down the ladder, taking each step carefully. He had rushed into action and he was wasting time. Travis fought hard to remain calm - he scoped the entire room. The good news was there was definitely no fire. Of that he was positive. It gave him a little reassurance.

He needed a plan. Taking a big breath, he looked around, and his eyes started focusing in the dark. Travis noticed that most of the lower seats had already been evacuated and as he scanned the carriage, he found a rolling set of stairs, just to the right of where Hank was standing on the outside circle.

"Hank, look back and to your right." Travis shouted down at him. "There's a set of stairs on rollers."

He watched as Hank reached the stairs. Then Travis literally jumped off the ladder and luckily landed both feet flat on the floor.

"Jeez, Travis. Anyway, I got the stairs." Hank was already rolling the stairs toward Travis. He stopped at a set of suspended chairs. The people in the chair started calling out to him.

Hank's next move was obvious so Travis asked, "Hank, can you handle the stairs by yourself?" Travis had to find a way to get to his Mom and Tara.

"I'm good, Travis." Hank set the stairs below a thankful couple and flipped the safety switch. He was relieved for more than one reason.

"I need to get higher." Travis said.

"Just don't do something stupid, Travis."

Travis didn't get a chance to respond. Luci came running up and in her excitement interrupted.

"Travis, there's a mechanical lift, near the back wall. It looks like they were trying to start it up to evacuate the high seats."

"That's great Luci, let's try to use it to get Mom and Tara."

Travis and Luci ran to the lift and they were lucky, the key was in the ignition. Travis climbed up into the bucket and found the screen on the lift was flashing. The staff had just run out and left it running!

"Here Travis, I can help." Luci was trying to read the instructions on the side. It was dark, so she used her teletab as a flashlight.

Travis poked at the flashing panel in futility. It wouldn't work? He couldn't get the screen to respond and the lift was frozen. What the heck? From beside him Luci's voice rose, "It says 'do not use if flashing. Travis, is the panel flashing?"

"Maybe." Travis answered very quietly to himself. "They are just trying to protect themselves; everything is going crazy and the same goes for this lift."

Much louder to Luci Travis answered, "No. It's not flashing."

"Let's push it across the floor." Travis said as he jumped out of the bucket and joined Luci on the ground. "We need to get this lift over to the center of the theatre."

Together they began pushing the lift towards the center of the room. Luci was trying to figure out how to fix it. She noticed the manual bar, which was fine for getting someone down, but lifting the bucket by hand was going to be tough, especially with Travis's big tuckus in it.

They finally got the lift to the docking station below Travis's Mom. Travis jumped back up on the lift, but they still couldn't get it to work.

"Luci, do something!" Travis was barking orders in his panic.

"I'm trying, Travis." Luci was randomly pressing buttons on the side panel of the lift.

Luci took a deep breath to calm down. They needed to set the brakes anyway she realized. She looked around, found the brake bar and pulled. Immediately, the light stopped blinking! That was it! The lift wouldn't work without the brakes being set!

Crossing her fingers, Luci reached up, turned on the lift and voila - it was fixed.

"I fixed it Travis, I got it." Luci shouted out. Travis was already in the bucket and ready to go. He was shouting over the soundtrack but Luci couldn't hear him. In frustration, Travis used the "OK" sign and thumbs up for 'lift'.

Luci responded with another thumbs up and activated the bucket's controls. As she watched, Travis disappeared like a shadow into the universe rising carefully into the seats. He realized too late that he was a seat over from his Mom and Tara. The man in that seat was more than pleased however.

"Thanks buddy. I was wondering how they were planning on getting us out of here." The man said as he looked up to see the young Travis in the light. "Wait - you're…"

"Welcome." Travis smiled. "You better get on if you're going down." As the man climbed into the bucket, Travis turned to his Mom and Tara and shouted. "I'll be right back. I promise."

He could see his Mom hugging Tara, not in a death grasp, but a comforting, round the shoulders type of hug. It looked like Tara had her eyes closed. As Travis and Luci brought the bucket down the man began asking questions.

"Where'd the staff go? There were probably five guys helping get the guests down and one guy working on the machine then suddenly they all left."

"I don't know what happened," Travis said, "There was a big boom from Mt. Alta and we saw them all run out the exit. That's when we came in. My friend Luci is running the lift and my friend Hank is down there operating the stairs."

"It was not very helpful, people got real anxious when everyone left. I was expecting the whole thing to blow or something. Seems silly, I know." the man added.

Travis shrugged. It didn't seem that silly to him. He was relieved to get the bucket down finally. The guy was right, something was really wrong. He needed to get Tara and his Mom off the ride.

"Thanks, kid…" The man reached out and shook his hand.

"Travis. My name is Travis."

"Thanks Travis, I'm Tommy." The man smiled and Travis shook his hand. As the man got out and slipped into the dark, Travis quickly, stepped out of the bucket and wiggled over to the controls where Luci was waiting.

"Luci, we need to move the lift over a little. To your right, let's try to position it over the next notch on the floor." Luci nodded and together they repositioned the crane. When Travis went up this time, the bucket was next to his Mom and Tara's chair.

"Look Ma! No hands" Travis rose beside them with both hands up in the air.

"Thanks Honey," Penelope Pruitt gave Travis a big smile. "Tara and I were fine really, but I appreciate you getting us out of here!" Mrs. Pruitt looked at the bucket carefully and made a quick decision.

"Travis, I think you should take Tara down first. I don't know how many that bucket is supposed to hold."

"We could try?" Travis started but Penelope shook her head.

"You take Tara down and then come back for me." She gave them both a reassuring smile. "I couldn't be prouder of both of you."

"Back into it Tara," Travis held the bucket up to the seat so it wouldn't move when she swung her legs over the railing. He could tell she was terrified, "Just don't look down."

Tara tugged on the seat belt but couldn't get it loose. It was safety locked! Looking around the side, Travis found a red button and reached out under the chair to push it.

"Got it…" Tara undid the belt but clung to the seat.

She slowly turned around and backed up towards the bucket moving first one hand, then the other, and finally swung a leg over the safety railing. Travis helped pull his sister into the lift and they began to descend. The rescue was quite heroic and all, but Tara was suspicious.

"What's up Travis?" Tara looked at him with big quiet eyes.

"The staffers are busy dealing with the park. It's kinda crazy out there."

"Why'd you come and get us?"

"We were nearby and I knew you were going to be here with Mom, so we just ran over."

"Travis. I know better. Something's up."

"I thought you might be scared. You know. What with the whole evacuation thing."

"You're lying about something. I get off of stuck rides all the time."

"Well, its park wide. I thought it might make you and Mom nervous."

"What's park wide? What do you know that you're not telling us?"

"OK. Promise you won't say anything? We've already gotten in trouble once today." Travis said quietly.

The crane made a sharp jerk to punctuate the statement and Tara clung to the sides to be sure not to fall. They had stopped. Travis looked over the bucket and could barely make out Luci below working with the control panel again.

"Honestly, we think there's an intruder in the park doing all this." Travis didn't often confide in Tara. It was mostly because they were so different, but, as long as they were stuck here like this, maybe Tara could help.

"How could the ride breaking down be an intruder? Wouldn't someone need to have access to the controls to make things go so crazy?"

Tara's eyes had grown bigger. Travis was a little embarrassed, Tara had already had more than one scare today and it wasn't really fair for him to frighten her more. But they needed to figure out how to stop this intruder!

Travis nodded. "Yes. I know. That is why it is so confusing. We think it might have something to do with the attack at security this morning."

Tara gave him a long angry look as she processed his answer.

"Travis, are you intentionally trying to scare me? You're starting to piss me off."

"Hear me out Tara. We don't think you are in any particular danger, we just think these things might all be connected. Think hard, please Tara, this morning, what exactly happened with that woman? Can you tell me a little more?'

"Well, it happened really fast. That woman reached over, grabbed me and sort of whispered "hang on kid." Then she just started screaming. She wasn't yelling at me though. It was like it was she was screaming at security the whole time. I was mostly scared by all the security officers and the fact that they wouldn't let Mom come over."

"I wondered why you were so calm."

"Yeah, I didn't want to focus on it too much." Tara said, as Travis nodded. "Plus, we were holding everyone up. And Mom was pretty mad; you know how she gets when she's worried about us. And she doesn't like uniformed people pushing her around much either."

"Yeah…" Travis laughed a little. His Mom didn't take to authority figures well.

"So I'm fine - but your story is crazy."

"Well, here's the thing. Luci saw a man run past the security gate at the same time you were attacked. She thinks the whole attack was staged to get him into the park. And I think she's right; at least there is a strange man on the park, we saw him climbing around on Mt. Alta and pulling on a circuit box. We've sort of been following him around, I mean, when we can find him. We don't know why or how, but we're pretty sure he's the reason all the attractions have gone crazy."

"Listen to yourself Travis. What you're saying doesn't make any sense. First, Luci - the conspiracy queen - comes up with this story about a planned attack and intruder. Second, what is the purpose of making things break down? You just get angry people. If the intruder was trying to shut down the park, he'd just cut the electricity and the whole park would shut down."

As Tara starting getting angrier, Travis turned and began working on the lift again. He was done with quality sibling time.

"More importantly Travis, what are you doing? You are going to get in so much trouble, and I can't believe I'm in this crane with you. Get me down this instant."

Almost on cue, the lift kicked on and Travis had them slowly descending again, through the floating chairs down to the concrete floor below them. Tara was silent as they came down and as they passed the second tier of chairs, Travis noticed guests climbing down the stair ladder and saw Hank moving the ladder from chair to chair. The lift jerked again, and Tara clasped the sides as

Travis looked down to see Luci was standing on the floor beside the crane. "No Wonder" He started to say, but then he recognized the man at the control panel as Tommy, the one he helped earlier.

"I figured I might as well help out." Tommy said to Travis.

"Sorry about that jolt Travis." Luci was waving, relieved to have them down. "It started flashing again and quit working but Tommy here helped me out. Hi, Tara!"

Tara didn't even respond. Instead, she quickly left the bucket and stepped over to the side to wait, arms crossed (and chin pointed) for her mother to be brought down.

Travis shook his head, letting Luci know it was useless to even try. Luci shrugged. She was used to Tara and Travis. She gave the operator a 'thumbs up' to head back up for Travis's Mom. When Travis and his Mom arrived back down, safe and sound, Tara was still standing, by the lift, mad as a hornet.

An uncomfortable silence took hold among the rescuers, even as Hank was coming back around with the rolling ladder. You didn't want to get between Tara and Travis in a standoff. Even Penelope Pruitt tried to steer clear. As she hopped out of the lift, Ms. Pruitt jumped into action.

"Here, let me help you out Hank." She said, and went to help Hank who was struggling to get the wheels of the rolling stairs aligned right.

In the dark, a good group of people were already down and milling about. Some left through the exit immediately, but others hesitated, and seemed to be looking for direction or waiting for an excuse to help out.

"Allow me." A man to the left of Travis offered to take over the bucket. "I used to work for the utility company; I know how to run these things."

Relieved, Travis also jumped out of the lift bucket and let the man take over.

"The girls in the next chair over are named Xophie and Monica." Tara told the new bucket man. "They may be scared to get in the lift. Tell them Tara already did it."

"Will do." The man said as the crane lifted up into the universe.

"Tara…" Travis tried to patch things up with her, but she interrupted him.

"Travis, we're safe on this park." Then she turned her back to him to watch as her friends greeted the bucket crane on its way up.

Wanting to break the tension, Luci came to Travis' rescue, "They've got this situation under control Travis. Let's go see what we can do to stop this."

A look of anger came over Tara's face. Travis didn't give her a chance to comment.

"Tara, you stay with Mom, OK?"

Tara didn't respond, instead she just turned her back towards Travis. Nearby, Hank and Mrs. Pruitt were pushing the ladder to a new chair.

"Hank, Luci and I were thinking of going back out into the park to see if we can find someone who can put a stop to this." Travis tried to act casual in front of his Mom. "Do you want to come with us?"

"Travis, you guys go on, I'm good here. I'll catch up with you later." Hank was feeling pretty comfortable so he added, "We really could use the help, Tara."

Luci hesitated but Travis was already a shadow in the dark headed to the lighted exit. She smiled and waved at Hank and took off after the shadow of Travis running into the light.

21

Intruders

"WHERE ARE WE HEADED?" Luci asked breathlessly when she finally caught up to Travis.

"Mt. Alta of course." Travis answered. "I thought that's what you meant."

"I was just trying to get you and Tara to quit fighting really." Luci said, "But, Mt. Alta is a good idea."

As Travis and Luci stepped into the plaza they were blinded by the daylight and hit a wall of people making the tedious journey to the front entrance. They were never going to make it through this crowd to Mt. Alta.

"Do you think we can get across by the zip line?" Travis was wondering how they could get across the Gad About lazy river.

"Well, there's no 'zip' going up hill from this side, but…" Luci laughed and paused thoughtfully, "You know there has to be some way for the staff to get to the main decks for maintenance, supplies, or trash removal."

"Yes! Trash removal –" Travis' face lit up. "Let's try the staff gate at the Conservatory. It's by the recycling lab. I've seen staff members with carts going in and out that door. There has to be something near there."

Travis and Luci ran across the plaza to Amy's Lab and just around the recycling bins they found a door marked 'Lab Researchers only.' It was obviously the Bee Plaza staff entrance. They tentatively pushed open the door and stepped through.

There were no alarms. No one stopped them. Incredibly, in the mass confusion throughout the park, they were able to pass undetected and undisturbed into the Staffer passage. It was a little nagging to Travis, but since they benefited, he didn't question it. Behind the door, there were evacuation paths painted on the floor and a small iron gate blocking a cement path in the direction of Mt. Alta. The gate wasn't locked and Luci and Travis followed it into a ventilated tunnel like corridor.

"Where are we?" Luci wondered. Her voice echoed in the tunnel. The walkway was dimly lit and you could hear the sound of large fans.

"I think we're inside that huge log that crosses the Gad About." Travis noted. "I never really thought about it, but it's got to be an access across the river."

"That's brilliant" Luci added. A lot of things were 'brilliant' on Hoverpark and Luci couldn't help but think this was a perfect system for an island.

As they walked along, the walkway suddenly opened up into a larger passageway. Travis had expected the corridor to end outside the volcano, but it seemed like they were - could it be?

"I'm pretty sure we're inside Mt. Alta, Travis!" Luci was in awe and a bit frightened. Alarms were going off but the place was practically deserted.

Travis couldn't help but be excited. He'd always wanted to know what was inside the volcano. And here he was! It was impressive; a vaulted room tucked inside a nest of trusses and thick cable stays. The walls were crisscrossed with pipes, duct work and a trash conduit. The center of the room was large clear tube like a giant aquarium. Travis noticed a control panel for releasing steam from the mouth of Mt. Alta. There were several winding metal stairways leading to rooms up above them and signs showing evacuation routes. They said "In Case of Emergency" in big red letters.

Each section of the park in fact was color coded. An entrance into Dr. Wren's Hover Lab at the Centrifuge in North Plaza was coded white. Vonderheist's west entrance through the hydroelectric dam was black. The door they came from, Amy's Bee Plaza was yellow and Ma Ridgely's courtyard was red. One wall was appropriately decorated with the Hoverpark Mission

Statement: "To encourage lifelong customer relationships and brand engagement through wondrous play and creative innovation. Hoverpark, Live the Wonder."

They didn't know which way to go but Luci stepped up to the yellow doorway and peeked down the hall. A large double door with a red first aid cross on it marked the staff hospital and through the glass windows you could see with several rooms. There was a lab, a radiology room, and a physical therapy studio arranged around a strangely large pool with a grated bottom. Across from the hospital, she could see computer panels, a line of scuba gear, wetsuits, tanks and lots of tools.

"Over here Luci," Travis whispered to get her attention. He was standing in front of a map and a sign reading 'Lower Decks." Travis and Luci followed the stairs down to the next level, where the door opened into another central great room. The walls were decorated with murals from ancient history including Mayan, Greek, Chinese, and Italian. Like above, each cardinal direction had a colored door. Travis peered around a black door and found a passage connecting several glass rooms filled with humming computers. Engineers were dashing through the stacks, pressing in codes and reading print outs. The room was chaotic, filled with voices on radios and occasionally someone would dash out a side door into another glass room. He stepped back unnoticed into the great room.

Through the red door, Travis and Luci crept past an empty staff break room and cafeteria. Several tables still had trays of food, and cups were scattered about in disarray. Travis couldn't help but notice that the food seemed much less appetizing than the meals up top in the park. The vending machines looked expensive too. He never thought about it before, but Hoverpark must be a tough place to work. Closed doors down that passageway had signs indicating they led to the dormitories on the lower decks where there was also a gym and a media room.

The hallway looped back out into the great room. Quickly scanning the room for staffers, Travis and Luci slipped into a third, white, door, where they found yet another hallway and a map. The maintenance elevator was clearly marked. It went to Orlop Deck and the navigation deck. Down the hall, they noticed a range of administrative offices and officer rooms. On the right was a stairway with a small sign that said "The Cave." Travis was elated!

"Luci, this is it. We've found the cave!" Travis whispered as they headed down the spiral staircase. "I can't believe it; we're finally visiting the cave!"

"We're breaking into the cave, Travis." Luci corrected him.

"Technically, we're lost." Travis laughed quietly. He wasn't going to let Luci destroy his moment of glory.

The walls around them appeared to be eroded limestone, and they were decorated with framed art and photos. They passed paintings of the portals, photos of a few vintage toggles and one photo of the 3-d printer in action with several executives standing around it. At the foot of the stairs, they stood quietly listening. In the distance they could hear voices. Someone was here! Cautiously Travis and Luci went on down the hall. There was only one way to go.

They crept down a small corridor, towards a lit doorway with actual plants growing on it. Roots, real and otherwise, intertwined around the door which was slightly ajar. Travis took several deep breaths. He had finally made it to the 'Cave,' the infamous home of the game master! From where they stood, Travis and Luci could see someone stepping into the light. Travis was so excited he could barely pay attention to what was happening around him. Luci shushed him and they slipped quietly against the wall towards the door. As they moved closer, they could hear voices. Shadows flashed as someone paced across the lighted doorway.

"What do you think you're doing? How did you get in here?" A deep voice shouted.

Travis and Luci froze in terror. How'd he see them? Then thankfully, another voice from inside the room answered.

"Don't be ridiculous. I belong here." A second voice responded.

Travis and Luci realized that must be the voice of the intruder! Travis and Luci weren't sure what was happening and they remained quiet hoping to figure it out.

"Not anymore you don't. You made your choice years ago." The first voice continued.

"What was I supposed to do?" said voice number two.

"You should have kept the faith. Look at this mess you created."

"Be realistic - You can't possibly think…."

"You want me to be realistic? Here's some realism for you. You are a beacon of mediocrity." The deep voice was brutally critical.

"Mediocrity? Now that's rich. It worked didn't it? I saw it through, which is more than I can say about you."

"I'm seeing it through as well. I'm planting ideas. Some may die, some may grow and flourish, but at least I tried. Hopefully the best ones will thrive."

"You don't know what, if any of it, will work."

"I know that - but it's worth the effort."

Travis and Luci couldn't stand the suspense and peeked carefully into the room, trying to see what was happening. One of the voices was obviously the intruder. Travis guessed the other voice, the deep one, was the game master. They slowly leaned in together, little by little, until they could just make out one of the men. The intruder it seemed was standing talking to the game master and he had a flannel shirt, khakis and dorky black shoes.

Travis' mouth opened just as Luci made a little gasp. It was the guy from the climbing wall!

Incredibly, their theory was right! Travis had met him, just before the fire on the Fracker! 'That explains a lot.' Travis thought and started trying to incorporate this new information into the plan. It was definitely him, but what were they going to do?

Suddenly, a noise behind them in the hallway startled them. In a quick-save stumble, they caught their balance, but Travis' clumsy elbow nudged the door which slowly squeaked open. All conversation stopped abruptly and Travis and Luci stood face to face with not one, but two men who looked exactly alike, they were identical twins!

22

Waltz of the Biotags

"Two?" Luci and Travis both blurted out.

They all four looked at each other briefly, shocked. Luci was visibly confused. It was all happening so fast! She wasn't sure what to do and she looked helplessly at Travis who was backing up slowly. Travis's mind was also whirling.

"Think, Think…" Travis mumbled to himself. What were they going to do?

And then, to their horror, both men jumped up and started after them! For a brief moment Luci considered fighting, but quickly decided her best bet was to run.

She could tell Travis had made the same split decision. Time stood still as Luci tried to remember how they got there. It was as if everything had slowed down so she could think clearly. She was mapping the path back to the park in her head. They had to clear the stairs first! Determined, Luci grabbed Travis's arm and turned to run. But just they as broke away, both men suddenly stopped!

The twins were looking at a point just over Travis and Luci's head. There was something behind them. The one twin, the game master, went and sat back down in the control seat. He turned to the computer and made a few more key strokes.

"Just stop right there," said a voice from behind them.

Curious, Travis took a quick glance over his shoulder. Beside him, Luci visibly jumped at the presence of Officer Cy Pinter.

"Stay right where you are." Cy said with calm authority.

Luci and Travis were relieved for a brief moment, and stepped toward Cy thankful that someone was there to handle the situation. They were quickly reprimanded.

"I said stay right where you are." Cy shot a nasty glance at them.

Shockingly, Travis and Luci realized that One-Eyed Cy was following **them!** They were out of their approved range, and he didn't know about the intruder! He had no idea, that is, until he saw the twins. Travis and Luci could see the shock on Cy's face as he recognized the situation.

Officer Cy Pinter became visibly angry. He was after the kids, but now there was something else. As Cy thought through the situation, a glooming silence implied order in the room.

"Don't anyone move a muscle." he said in frustration. "And that includes you George."

Cy was carefully taking stock of the situation, but he hesitated slightly and that's when the intruder jumped in to 'explain.'

"Cy, it's me, Winston." He explained, but he was immediately interrupted by the seated twin.

"Thank goodness you're here Cy, George just came barging in...right before these kids." The seated twin said quickly indicating Travis and Luci who stepped back defensively.

"No, Cy, I'm Winston. My brother has…"

"Oh, come on!" The seated twin started. "You come charging in here, making all kinds of demands…" He looked at Cy to see how things were going.

Officer Cy was thinking. He looked back at the twins, Travis and Luci, thinking.

"Cy," The seated twin continued hands outstretched, "You can't seriously believe him - after working with me for years? For goodness sakes, we both had oatmeal for breakfast this morning; you like fresh peaches and Mable had some delivered yesterday. Hal and Mike have been working on a blown circuit today which has shorted out some of the systems. In fact, I'm guessing George (the seated twin indicated the one with black shoes) is probably responsible for the fire that started this mess."

The standing twin tried to respond. "Cy, this is ridiculous. Can't you tell the difference? You can't honestly believe?"

"That's enough." Cy interrupted him. He had settled down into his heels. You could see his mind turning, and he had chosen the seated twin.

"George, you have been banned from this ship and all Hoverpark properties." Cy stood up straighter and puffed his chest out as he continued. "You are officially trespassing and I'm putting you under arrest until the authorities can arrive. You can come quietly or I can call for reinforcements."

The intruder twin lifted his hands and stepped calmly towards Cy who was startled. Luci couldn't help wondering why he would volunteer to come so calmly. If he was the same intruder who had caused such chaos, why would he be so cooperative?

"You kids come with me as well." Cy nodded. With much dismay, Travis and Luci joined him and the four of them headed out the door, leaving the seated twin alone in the room.

"Thanks Cy, for taking care of that. I'll give Tampa Police a call." The seated twin called out to them as they left.

"That'd be great Winston." Cy called back at him. "Let's go George."

Almost immediately the alarms went silent, and as they walked back up the stairs and through the black door to the security office, Travis and Luci noticed staffers opening locked cabinets, checking monitors and entering codes so the park could run smoothly again. On the left, was a huge room was filled with rows of computers, blinking and buzzing, Technicians were plowing through the stacks, entering code and rebooting.

The security office was just down the hall, and to the right. Cy opened the door and escorted all of them into a large room. On the right was a neat sitting area, two desks, a few locked cabinets, and a large monitor with multiple views of the park. On the left were two small holding cells. The black shoed George practically walked himself into the holding cell and Cy went to code up the door. Cy's dog was asleep in his kennel, his work collar hanging on a hook above it, and he woke up as they entered, his tail wagging. He wasn't much of a watchdog.

Luci stopped to look inside a narrow trophy case which held framed awards, certificates, letters and an occasional old paper clipping. She started reading the letters of appreciation in the case and noticed a familiar looking newspaper clipping, framed with a letter from the Governor of Florida. The article was about the kid who saved the families in Orlando. Intrigued, Luci tried to focus closer on the letter but she was interrupted by Cy as he went around the desk and searched his drawers.

"I don't have time for you kids." He was obviously flustered at the turn of events and having to deal with Travis and Luci. He slammed the drawer shut and stared.

"What do you have to say for yourselves?" He asked.

Travis and Luci both answered at once. "We were looking for the intruder." "We were just trying to stop him."

"Silence." Cy barked, interrupting them. "That's enough. I've got to focus on security for the operations. Things on deck are a mess. And I've got to meet with the Tampa Police Department." He trained his eye on first Travis, then Luci, and back to Travis who seemed to get an extra glint of hate from the Security Chief.

"You shouldn't have come inside here." Cy added, "I should kick you off the park. In fact, that's exactly what I'm going to do."

Travis almost fainted. He looked at Luci, then back at his shoes. He started to protest but then he lost his nerve. Luci put her hand on his shoulder to stop him from reacting. She knew what angry adults were like, she knew to be quiet and obey, to be small as a mouse.

"You two come with me." Cy barked, and he turned to leave.

Before he could take a step however, George the intruder in the holding cell called out to him.

"I'm telling you Cy, you're making a big mistake."

"Shut up." Cy said and he slammed both his hands down on the desk. "Tampa police will be here shortly and you'll be taken to the county jail."

"Hear me out Cy, please."

"No. I'm done with you. You've done enough harm for the day. You sneak onto this park, start a fire and create total chaos, and you want me to listen to you? You - arrogant jerk - you've created so much extra paperwork on this ship and you did it on purpose. You've disrupted operations for hours and God only knows what kind of follow up I'm going to have to do to prevent this from happening again. In fact you had better shut up or I swear, I'll shoot you myself."

Cy dismissed the jailed intruder and motioned again to Travis and Luci to follow him. He started to step out the door but then he turned to face George.

"I always hated you - you and your brother. You are smug little arrogant pustules. You thought the whole park was all about you. You're both spoiled, self-serving jerks - your brother just wears it better." Cy paused suddenly. His frustrations were obvious, and he turned with vehemence to Travis and Luci.

"I need to focus. And I don't have time for you." Cy spat out angrily.

He started towards the door again, and then stopped and turned around to look at them. Travis and Luci were silent. 'Don't poke the angry bear' Luci said to herself. She even crossed her fingers. With a nod, he indicated that they follow him. Travis and Luci were reluctant, but they almost had to run to keep up with Cy. They were going so fast, they nearly missed running into the game master as he was coming down the hall.

"Cy!" He called out in a friendly tone. "I just wanted to let you know Tampa Police Department is on the way."

Cy glared. "I'll meet them at the service entrance."

"Do you mind Cy?" The game master indicated the office with the holding cell. "I haven't seen George in over 10 years. I feel sorry for him."

Cy stared furious, seething. But then it appeared he saw no good reason not to honor his request.

"OK." Cy took a breath. "You can go on inside. But don't feel too sorry for him. He got himself in this mess." In distraction, Cy turned back around and continued down the hall, mumbling to himself.

"Sorry little pompous twerps." Cy added, speaking through his teeth to himself.

He'd practically forgotten about Travis and Luci. They passed the original operations room, when one staffer, noticing them from the other side of the glass, came running up to Cy.

"Cy, we're not getting any feedback from the duty manager at GENsys. They haven't checked in yet."

"Just get it started again. Get this park running before people start getting violent." Cy spat at him

Travis started - then stopped - looking at Luci. They wanted to protest, they knew what was happening but if they said something Cy would definitely flip out. Helpless they exchanged looks of fear. Luci knew more about violent, crazy adults. She gently shook her head at Travis as a warning. They would just have to trust the others to know what to do. They had no choice.

As they followed him, they realized, incredibly, Cy was walking them out the exit route. Luci recognized the artwork on the wall. Suddenly Cy turned to face them, his eye patch visibly twitching in anger.

"I assure you this is not my best decision, but I am releasing you back into the park. Do not return to these decks, you will not get another chance." Cy stood up tall and adjusted his belt, trying to look as authoritative as possible.

"I don't need to tell you this story doesn't go beyond these corridors do I?" Cy glared at Luci and Travis, commanding their total attention. He ominously pointed his finger at them and added, "I have the ability to block you from the Hoverpark, you understand?"

Luci and Travis nodded. They understood completely. Travis actually quivered under an imaginary laser gun which he thought might be behind Cy's eye patch.

In silence, Cy walked them into the center of the Hovership and down another hall again towards the exit. From the looks of things, the park had calmed down significantly. Staffers were walking down the hall, staring at them.

As they continued towards a red exit sign, suddenly their teletabs rebooted and without fail, Ms. Edison's monitoring flashed across Travis's and Luci's teletabs.

"Crap" they both said at once.

Cy exploded in anger and frustration.

"What now?" He growled, his pocked nostrils flared with each breath.

"We can't stop it. It's our biotags." Travis was helpless and defeated in this latest development. He was going to lose his biotag. Cy was going to kick him off the park forever.

"You could tell her it's OK?" Luci quietly suggested to Cy. She didn't look him in the eye.

Why would I do that? You shouldn't have snooped around where you weren't wanted. I would have caught - I did catch - George, without the help of any kids." Cy gave them a glare insisting that that agree.

"Yes, you did." Travis said. "And we really appreciate that."

"Don't try to butter me up boy." Cy's one eye flashed with sudden anger.

Ms. Edison's call blasted over their teletabs again, insisting.

"She knows where we are." Luci said a little boldly.

Abruptly, Travis and Luci were roughly pushed back out the service entrance which led to the Conservatory in Bee Plaza. Suddenly, Cy grabbed both of them by the back of their shirts and jerked them backwards. Luci almost fell over. Cy snatched their teletabs out of their hands, scanned them with his security wand, and typed in a code. The alarm went silent and both of their teletabs rebooted again. Luci turned to thank him, but the door was closed, leaving them outside of Amy's Conservatory.

The sun was glaring and its brightness blinded them. Travis and Luci were standing still, letting their eyes adjust.

"Wow." Travis took a deep breath. "That was close."

"No kidding." Luci added. "Cy really is a jerk."

"Mostly." Travis said.

There was a moment of silence. Then Luci broke the quiet.

"Travis," Luci hesitated, "You were right about the intruder. I mean, earlier today, when we refused to believe you." Travis glanced around anxiously in the conservatory. "I'm sorry, Trav" Luci said.

"I don't think we should talk now." He said, indicating a camera hanging from the ceiling. Luci nodded and together they left the building.

"Thanks though." Travis gave Luci a friendly punch in the shoulder and smiled.

The plaza was full of people, all rushing somewhere. Travis paused to look around and Luci stepped up beside him. They were interrupted by another call from Ms. Edison.

"What is going on? Where are you? I got a biotag alert and then it disappeared." Ms. Edison asked.

"We don't know Ms. Edison," Luci started. "We're in Bee Plaza and our teletabs just rebooted. I think it was the old alert? Must be a glitch."

"You've snuck by on this one Luci, but I'm warning you! Do not make my day any worse." Ms. Edison's patience was slim. "Furthermore, you are not in your group of three. You are closest to Mrs. Pruitt who you will find on your map at the GENsys. I want you and Travis to locate her immediately."

"Yes, Ms. Edison." She closed the call and Luci and Travis were alone again, silent.

"I wonder what's happening at the GENsys.?" Luci mumbled out loud.

"We're getting ready to find out." Travis was looking across the plaza at the crowds of parkers exiting the GENsys.

23

Meanwhile

Back at the GENsys Tara was furious with Travis. He always took decisions, making them for everyone. And he didn't even try to consider what might be the simplest solution, especially if there was an opportunity for adventure. He was reckless, self-centered and everyone loved him for it. When Luci and Travis had left, she refused to speak to him. But she watched them leave, two dark silhouettes against a lighted door. And it scared her.

"We could really use help, Tara" Hank interrupted her thoughts.

Turning her back to Travis' shadow, Tara nodded at Hank and stepped up to help with the evacuation of the GENsys. It was more chaotic than she thought. Several adults were 'helping' with the evacuation now. Hank and Penelope were still rolling the stairs around the floor from seat to seat, but people on the floor kept trying to direct their efforts. On the lift, Tommy was at the control panel trying to guide several adults to shift the lift up to the left and over again until they hit another mark on the floor but no one was listening.

"This one is higher" Tara heard someone yell from the bucket, and almost immediately afterward there was a chorus of angry parkers shouting, 'what about me', 'you skipped us' and 'don't just leave us here.'

They needed to evacuate in an order to keep people calm. It was taking too long and people were starting to get angry. After much hand gesturing, and yelling Tara watched some of the extra adults sulk off. Tommy had the controls again and as the bucket lifted up, another guy tried to shout instructions down to the floor. Tara watched the bucket lift finally make it to Xophie and Monica. It was taking them a little while to come down. Not knowing what to do, Tara stepped in on the other side of the rolling stairs with her Mom and Hank.

"Honey, let's get this moved over to the next tier." Penelope motioned to the next set of marks. As she pushed, the stairs into place she saw first Xophie, then Monica make it down on the lift and start looking around for her on the floor.

Tara considered running off and joining them, but it was obvious Hank and her Mom could really use her help. It would be rude to just take off anyway. Tara was pulling out her teletab to try to contact them, but then the whole room went black. The lights went out, the movie screen went blank, even the emergency lights were dimmed - everything completely shut down!

There was a sudden brief silence, then screams. The chairs had settled down into a lock mode but everyone thought they were falling! In the darkness, with the screaming and confusion, Tara almost started to panic but suddenly the lights came back on. It helped that people could see around them. Monica and Xophie for instance, finally found Tara and stood by shyly to assist with the stairs.

"Look, Monica and Xophie are here so you've got the stairs, I'm going to go help Tommy with the lift OK?" Hank suddenly took off towards the inside of the rotunda to find Tommy.

As the parkers, still dangling in their seats, started looking down in the light, they grew more anxious. They could see the floor, and the mechanics holding up the chairs, and it made them nervous. People could also see the evacuation efforts, and they started yelling for Tara to help them get down. Then a voice began counting down over the speaker system and the room went dark again as the screens flashed.

With a slow creak, the mechanics started shifting the chairs into place in the dome and the movie began again. Tara took stock of the situation. Alarmed, it occurred to her the GENsys had rebooted. Tara realized they needed to get out of the way before the chairs started coming back down to the floor!

"Mom - why isn't the safety stopping the ride? With all these people on the floor, the floor sensors at least should be going off and stopping it?" Tara asked.

"I don't know honey, you're right though; we need to get off the floor." In a steady push, Penelope started rolling the stairs towards the walls as fast as possible. Monica and Xophie joined her at the back of the stairs and started pushing as well.

"Hank, Tommy!" Tara called out into the dark. "Get out of there! You have to move the lift out and fast."

It was so loud they couldn't hear her. Tara could see that they were working on it, but not fast enough. She knew the script to the GENsys by heart. They already had passed the storm and reached the part where, by accident, you are tossed into the spiral of Orion's arm. The ether screen maps were up, letting the parkers explore and compare star clusters in search of Earth's solar system. Looking at the closest screen, Tara could identify the actual footage of Sirius and Procyon. By her estimates, they had three minutes at the most to move the lift out.

"Mom - the lift - I'm going to help. I'll be back." Tara took off running towards the lift.

For a minute Penelope considered running after her and leaving the stairs to Monica and Xophie, but one look at the doe eyed terror in the girls' eyes convinced her otherwise.

"Tara, you be careful." It was all Penelope could muster to say. Her daughter was going into the dark and in seconds she was gone. Penelope struggled inside, but threw all her concern into pushing the stairs.

"Hank, Hank!" Tara could just barely see the lift, like a shadow under the moving chairs and she ran toward it. "Hank," she said again.

"Hey, Tara." Hank was happy to see her though he was a bit surprised. "Tara, this is Tommy. Remember him?"

"Hi." Tara politely dismissed the introduction. "Listen guys, we don't have time. You have to move the lift off the floor now."

"We're trying to but see, the thing is, the lift has shut down completely. The brakes are set and we can hardly get it to budge." Hank explained, "Tommy and I both have been pushing it. And Willy up there is stuck in the bucket."

"Howdy." Willy shouted down at Tara, waving. The movie moved past a distant view of Earth's solar system, and headed instead to explore Barnard's Star and Cygni. Tara ignored Willy. Enough with this 'hello' business, they did not have time.

"Did you try turning it on? Is there a key?" Tara understood immediately. When the system rebooted, it rebooted the lift as well. Normally, she would find it interesting that the emergency equipment was linked to the park's computer systems but right now she needed to focus on getting it started.

"It's a keypad. We don't know the code." Hank pointed to the keypad and shrugged as Tommy pushed with his whole weight against the lift. It slid about two inches. The wheels wouldn't roll at all.

Tara stood in silence in front of the keypad thinking hard. "We need the code. Where's Travis? He could…." Tara realized, with all the weight of the fact, it was just her.

"No," she said to herself, "Travis can't. He's not here. It's just you Tara. Think. Think."

Every second counted. Tara saw the brilliant Altair galaxy in the distance. She looked at the keypad and realized it was just numbers, so that was good. There was room for seven. Tara started punching in random codes. First she tried 1234567. No. She tried the date the park opened. No. Concentrating, she tried others. No and no. As she typed, she thought about the layout of the ride. How the line wove around the rotunda similar to a nautilus shell and how the chairs come down to rest in spirals on the floor. Like flower petals. Of course! The Fibonacci code - quickly she typed '0112358' and heard the buzz of the lift as it activated. Yes! Like magic, the bucket started coming down again, with Willy celebrating as it tried to settle into the lift. Above him, she saw Alpha Centauri and realized that soon the chairs would be responding to a solar flare.

"There's not time to wait, we have to move it out to the walls, now." Tara shouted.

Tommy released the brakes and threw his shoulder into the lift. Thankfully the wheels turned smoothly, and the lift started rolling out. Willy shouted out and Tommy answered for him to 'Hold on.' Once the lift was moving…it just kept rolling, faster and faster as they ran…and it was about time.

The chairs were 'gliding' through the solar system at this point preparing to zoom back into 'earth' on the floor. The music was in a grand crescendo! What was wrong with Hank? Tara saw Hank hesitating, he was just standing there admiring the moving lift and waving at Willy! Tara's heart was beating with the timpani as the drums slowed down to highlight the 'landing'. They had almost four bars left!!! She ran back, grabbed Hank's hand and together they sprinted to the outside wall.

Two, two, three, two, four, two - the drums beats rolled and then the music ended. Boom. Tara and Hank made the edge of the loading dock just as the room went dark. She turned around to face the center of the room, the direction they came from. Did Tommy and Willy make it? The mechanics started whirling as the chairs descended and exit lights slowly brightened. In the twilight of the rotunda floor, they could see the lift still rolling out towards the wall, Willy crouching down in the bucket and Tommy running behind the whole shebang. Feet dangled above them as the chairs swooped down behind them and started docking in the center. Tommy kept on plowing the lift towards the edge. A child's foot just slipped past the bucket and Willy's hand as the lift moved into safety. Behind it, two rows of feet barely grazed Tommy's head. Finally, Tommy, head ducked down, cleared the floor. The chairs docked and with a loud click, the seat belts snapped open and parkers started filling the exit doors.

Tara realized she hadn't been breathing at all. In fact, what she thought was her own breathing, was Hank panting beside her. Relaxing, finally, she looked turned to the beaming group beside her. There were quick high fives all around with Tommy and Willy. And then, much to her surprise, Hank gave Tara a big bear hug, that even picked her feet up off the ground!

It was a brief celebration. Staffers had come back inside through the open doors and were quickly escorting them out of the building along with the other parkers. They probably would have gotten into a significant amount of trouble, but none of the staffers wanted to fill out the paperwork, or explain why they had left the building. They were busy enough as it was.

24

Together

"**Y**ou did it Tara! You figured it out!"

Outside in the gardens, Hank was telling an impressed Penelope, Xophie and Monica all about how Tara cracked the code and saved the day. She was quite embarrassed in fact, but proud, and she didn't avert her eyes when Travis and Luci joined them. It was a happy reunion. As Hank shared the story of Tara's brilliant rescue, Penelope chimed in and added her version of the chairs sweeping down over Tommy's head, and the way Tara had grabbed Hank and ran - it was quite dramatic, especially when Mrs. Pruitt added the lighting and sound effects of the movie. Travis was particularly interested in how Tara cracked the code.

"What was the code Tara? How did you figure it out?"

"I just tried some numbers." Tara answered modestly.

"And?" Travis loved cracking codes.

"It was the Fibonacci sequence. You know, the pattern of nature?"

Tara looked around and saw only blank faces, all of them waiting for her explanation.

"No, I don't know." Hank answered for Travis who was stunned silent.

"It's a pattern of numbers; each number is the sum of the two numbers before it. So, the sequence starts one, one, and the next number is two, then after that, three and then five - get it?"

"Ok. I see the pattern. But why would you even think of that?"

"Well, it's pretty popular among math nerds and, you know, engineers. It is named after Fibonacci, an Italian mathematician from the Middle Ages, who used it to explain patterns in nature like flower petals and seeds for instance in a sunflower. So, if you count the number of spirals in a sunflower, you'll find numbers from the sequence. There may be eight or thirteen spirals for example, but not seven. Anyway, if you look around in the GENsys, you'll see it does the same thing."

Tara explained. "So, I tried the Fibonacci sequence and it worked."

Everyone was silently impressed. Travis shrugged at Luci, they were both in awe. The silence was broken by Xophie who chimed in, "Who knew history could be so useful?"

"I know, right?" Monica lilted and she and Xophie laughed together.

Luci stared. She couldn't believe anyone could be that stupid.

"Tara, you are fabulous!" Monica added and Tara smiled a bit broader.

Everyone else looked at the trio a little strange, but the good mood was infectious.

As the rush over the recent drama slowly passed, Penelope Pruitt's attention shifted to Travis and Luci.

"And where were you and Luci during this dramatic interlude?" she asked, eyebrows raised.

"Luci and I were trying to find help."

"Did you find the door? Did you go inside Mt. Alta?" Hank interrupted, even as Luci shot him the stink eye. It was too late. Travis had smiled, just a little bit and Tara caught it.

"Travis! Did you seriously go below deck in Mt. Alta?" Tara asked pointedly.

"Yes, well, maybe?" Travis said, looking around at everyone's reaction; looking around especially at his Mom's reaction.

"But how did you get past all the security?" Tara asked.

"It was easy actually," Travis said, "All the gates were down and people were too busy to say anything to us."

"You just walked back there? Nobody stopped you? What about the Geotags?" Tara bombarded him with questions.

"The computers were down, remember? We just walked back there, no problem. Everything's fine."

"And?" Tara stared Travis, demanding for the story.

"And, what?" He tried to appear nonchalant. His Mom stood behind Tara, also waiting.

"You know what, Travis."

"No, I don't."

"Yes, you do." Tara had one her sassy browed stare of girlydom. "What did you learn about the 'alleged' intruder?" There was an audible gasp from Xophie and Monica at the word 'intruder'.

"What? What intruder?" Xophie asked as she looked around confused at the general group. She finally settled on Hank, "What is she talking about?"

"I don't know." Hank answered her on the side. He shook his head and shrugged but watched Travis closely. Travis was looking at his shoes trying not to make eye contact.

"Travis," Mrs. Pruitt interrupted loudly, taking over the interrogation. "I thought we were going to drop that wild goose chase?"

"Mom…." Travis started to make excuses but he was cut off.

"Did you, or did you not, run off to chase this imagined bit of drama you've got no business pursuing?" There was an uncomfortable silence.

"Yes, we did and I'm sorry." Luci jumped in to help. "We're real sorry Mrs. Pruitt. We were worried, and we did go inside Mt.

Alta. We shouldn't have done it. But we found Officer Cy Pinter and he has complete control over the security of this park."

"One eyed Cy?!" Xophie's eyes grew big. She whispered at Hank, "Did she just say they ran into One-eye Cy in the Cave?" Hank nodded a silent response. He was watching everyone very closely.

Mrs. Pruitt was not impressed and continued to stare Travis down. Travis tried his hardest to act sorry, but Penelope Pruitt wasn't convinced. She stared. Finally Travis had to say something.

"I'm sorry Mom. I was trying to help, honest. Everyone was stuck on the GENsys and there was so much going on. I really thought - well, Luci is right. We did find Officer Pinter and he brought us back out, but it's OK. We're not in trouble."

"Travis?" Mrs. Pruitt asked again. She knew her son and he seldom let it go when he got an idea in his head.

"It's dropped Mom. I promise. It's over." Travis said emphatically. And it was over. The intruder was in custody and Tampa Police Department was on its way.

"The difference between an adventure and a nightmare is whether or not you can let it go when you need to Travis." Mrs. Pruitt gave him 'the Look' and paused for effect.

"It's over Mom." Travis said it again and smiled weakly. Penelope Pruitt smiled back, reached over and ruffled his hair. Travis was embarrassed but glad she wasn't mad anymore.

"That's good, honey." She said. "We've had quite a day." And everyone nodded a sigh a relief. It had been quite a day indeed.

25

QUESTIONS

"So, what's the plan? Where are we headed next?" Hank started to ask but was abruptly interrupted by an alarm on all of their teletabs.

It was Ms. Edison of course; demanding a mini meeting among the chaperones, to debrief about the shutdown. They hear Mrs. Torez complaining about the geotags, and recommending everyone stay in a group. Penelope Pruitt frowned a bit at that, the park had rebooted obviously, and everything appeared to be OK, which is what she told them. Almost to accentuate her point, they could hear the parkers screaming on the Vonderheist and Mt. Alta released a puff of 'volcanic' smoke.

"Well, is everyone accounted for?" Ms. Edison asked.

"Yes, yes, they're all here," Ms. Pruitt and Mrs. Torez started to say but Mrs. Nash interrupted them.

"Well no, not everyone." Mrs. Nash said. "I'm missing three students." "I'm still missing Dustin, Tosh and Mel." Mrs. Nash said. Over the noise of all three chaperones searching for clues among their students, Penelope Pruitt turned back to her group.

"Ok, we're still missing Dustin and his two friends. Do any of you remember anything that might help us find them?" She asked.

"You mean, other than the fact that they are jerks?" Hank answered, but then added, "We saw them earlier on the Gad About. They're probably still in the water somewhere and have their teletabs turned off in a locker." He couldn't believe he'd just helped Dustin!

Mrs. Pruitt made the call. "Ok, let's head over to the Cenote and fan out along the Gad About. We need to find Dustin and his friends."

"Ugghhh! Now we're stuck on some rescue mission for the meanest bully in school!" Travis couldn't help mumbling as they plodded off. "What a waste of our time."

Crossing the plaza was even worse than earlier. The crowds were massive. It was hot. And a lot of parkers were calling it a day and leaving. They were trailing along together in tight knit lines like ant highways making it virtually impossible to break through. To stay together, Tara, Xophie and Monica held hands as they tried to dodge through the crowd following Travis and Mrs. Pruitt. Over the loud speakers, a pleasant voice was giving directional assistance.

"Due to high traffic, support transportation back to the parking deck is available at the hot air balloon docks."

They could see the tops of hot air balloons rising just above the horizon of the park, like giant colorful mushrooms growing. The balloons were ominous in a way, with their puffs of fiery smoke and the sound of whooshing as they rose. It made the whole park look like a Victorian street carnival. Thankfully, they were traveling in the opposite direction from the exiting crowds, going towards Mt. Alta. Travis and Penelope made it across the plaza first and they waited, watching the others weave through the crowds.

"So, did Ms. Edison say we have to leave the park after we find Dustin?" Travis was afraid Ms. Edison was going to cut their field trip short.

"No. Ms. Edison didn't say anything about leaving. Don't worry, we still have more time to play. The buses aren't supposed to be back at the park until after 7:30 anyway, so we wouldn't get very far even if we did leave."

"Good. I really would hate to miss the finale."

"Me too, kiddo." Ms. Pruitt tussled Travis' hair affectionately much to his chagrin.

Further behind them, Hank was clinging to Luci as they dove in and out through the crowd. Hank was trying to talk to her about the Mt. Alta, but she kept avoiding it.

"Not now." Luci said between her teeth as she pushed into the crowd behind Xophie. Hank dragged along next to her.

"But what happened?" Hank was starting to get a bit angry.

"We'll have to tell you later." Luci whispered and jerked her head in the general direction of Mrs. Pruitt. It was a gesture Hank was familiar with, so it worked. But he could barely contain himself; he was itching all over with wanting to know.

They all stopped on the bridge to look over the crowd in the Gad About. It was fairly calm, no Dustin at all. Tara pointed out a triangle of numbers next to the Eye of Horus on the wall lining the river.

"Check it out, its Pascal's Triangle," Tara said. "I wonder why they have all these magic math patterns here. Probably because the engineers were a bunch of math geeks."

"What exactly is that triangle?" Luci asked, curious. "It looks familiar, but I'm not sure what it is."

"Pascal's Triangle could be lots of things. Each number in the pyramid is the sum of the numbers above it. But there are lots of patterns in it. So, if you add each row together, for instance, it makes numbers that can be divided by two."

"That's pretty smart Tara." Travis was impressed. "For a girl." He was joking but it didn't go over well.

"Quit being such a jerk Travis." Luci stepped in and put her arm around Tara. "It's highly possible, she is the good twin."

Travis winced. The girls were getting on his nerves. Boss…y. He marched off the bridge, swinging a left towards the Cenote. There was the laughter of wild abandon as guests jumped into the open pool to greet the clouds below them. From the overlook, you could see perfectly through the clear bottom of the Cenote into the gulf. It looked like the tide was going out. A dark swath of wet sand below was growing larger and the waves were swirling backwards in frothy circles.

Penelope Pruitt gathered them up.

"I'm staying here as command central." Mrs. Pruitt said. "We need two groups to take either direction of the Gad About."

In her new confidence, Tara boldly took off to the North with Xophie and Monica. Luci considered joining them but instead, somewhat reluctantly, went with Travis and Hank to the South. They walked together in an uncomfortable silence. Travis was visibly tense. Hank was beside himself wanting to know what happened on Mt. Alta; and Luci was, well, Luci was tired of the boys right now.

Passing through a row of lounge chairs, Luci carefully rubbed the back of a chair and then pulled out her teletab to tag it.

"What is that about?" Hank took the bait.

"It's made of recycled plastics. It is something I read about when I was doing research for Citizens against Hover Park. They have these large 3-D printers here that use recycled base, so practically everything you see is created by recycled materials."

"Seriously?" Travis spat out the word angrily. "You are seriously still working on our homework Luci?"

"Travis! What the heck is wrong with you?" Hank stepped over to Luci who stood her ground, ready for battle.

"You don't know the half of it." Travis snapped back.

"No I don't. But whose fault is that? I mean, what the heck Travis, if anybody has a reason to be mad it's me. Are you going to tell me what happened or not?" Hank said sullenly.

It was a face off; with all three raring to take on the challenge. The tension was high, especially since Travis and Luci knew they needed to be careful. Luci was a little guilty. And most importantly, Hank was their friend. He had been with them throughout this whole ordeal and Hank needed to be updated.

Travis looked at his best friends and nodded.

"Let's go look for Dustin over by that loud waterfall." Travis said but he indicated he wanted to talk about much more than Dustin.

Thankfully, they understood and followed him along the lifeguard path beside the Gad About. They passed a lifeguard talking on an internal phone line, and found a spot next to a scenic, but loud, waterfall.

"Point down the river." Travis directed.

Hank was getting tired of the secrecy, and the bossiness, but Travis gave him the eye and he pointed. As they pretended to look up and down the river, Travis and Luci quickly and quietly shared their adventure below deck inside Mt. Alta. The told Hank about finding the cave, the twins, Cy and Ms. Edison.

"So there really was an intruder?" Hank asked. He'd believed their protests earlier.

"Oh, yes. Cy took him into custody."

"So, it's over?" Hank asked.

"It looks like it's over. The park's fine; I mean everything is running smooth, right?" Travis asked Luci.

"It looks like it." Luci looked at Travis a bit tentatively.

"What's the problem?" Hank was still confused. "If the intruder is captured…?"

"Well, it was a little weird. The intruder insisted *he* was the game master." Luci explained to Hank. "But he was obviously the one who broke into the park. We recognized him as the guy who we've been following. Most importantly, after he was caught, the park settled down so it makes sense." She agreed with Travis.

"Except -" Luci went slowly. She didn't want to be the bearer of bad news but this was important.

"I'm pretty sure he was the one who helped us get Travis out of the malfunctioning portal today." Luci said and looked at them, hoping they wouldn't be mad.

Travis knit his brows slightly, thinking.

"Really?" Hank looked puzzled. "But didn't we figure that was the game master this morning?" Hank said.

"Yeah." Luci said.

"But if…?" Travis stopped confused. Then he noticed the lifeguard looking over at them.

"We've got to quit talking." Travis said, nodding over in the direction of the lifeguard. Now was definitely not the time to share. The lifeguard was watching them and talking on the internal phone line.

With enthusiastic random pointing, they continued looking out over the Gad About until Luci suddenly broke the silence.

"Over there - I see them - Dustin and his friends!" Luci was pointing in the direction of a 'raft' of floating teenagers shouting at a group of cannons spouting water at the Gad About. Dustin and his friends were blocking the water flow and hiding behind the cannons only to release it as parkers floated by. You could see Dustin's big head practically bobbing off his body with laughter.

"What jerks." Luci said, preaching to the choir.

Travis was on the teletab to Mrs. Pruitt immediately, and they got to enjoy the vision of Ms. Edison rising like Godzilla over the cannons across the river, behind Dustin and his friends, and directing them to the lockers. Dustin kicked a solar tree as he stormed off, which was funny. It didn't budge at all and it looked like he stubbed his toe pretty bad.

"Poor Dustin." Hank laughed.

"Poor Dustin, indeed." Luci added.

"Mom says to meet back up with her on the overlook. She says its time to eat." Travis was still talking to his mom on the teletab.

"It's about time," Hank chimed in, visibly happier as they walked back up the path towards the Cenote.

RELAXING

"It's my treat kids." Penelope Pruitt offered as they stood around the menu at the Cenote Cafe. The smell of burgers, plaintain and fresh chips wafted in the air. As luck would have it, the line for food was basically open, since everyone had eaten during the brownout.

"I always liked your Mom, Travis." Hank said and he ordered a hamburger, all the way, with chips.

Penelope Pruitt was a sweetheart by anyone's estimate. They found a large table for six overlooking the Gad About, it was a fine place to have an early dinner. They could watch parkers splash around and relax a bit before going back to the rides. It was a perfect dinner spot, very relaxing.

Xophie and Monica nibbled on salads and rated boys as they floated by, using a random point system.

"Thanks again for dinner, Mrs. Pruitt" Luci said.

"You're welcome Luci," Penelope Pruitt said and then opened up a new dinner conversation.

"So, what was it like? Inside Mt. Alta?" She asked.

"It's fabulous. Travis answered her. "It looks kinda like a cruise ship but with lots of computers and tools. There are huge aquariums decorating the walls with fish I don't even recognize!"

"They have an onboard clinic with a lab," Luci added. "There's a surgery suite and a pool for physical therapy - there's even radiology equipment. You'd like it Mrs. Pruitt."

"It sounds like I would, Luci." Penelope Pruitt laughed. "I have to admit I'm jealous. Maybe one day I'll get to go behind the scenes." She took another bite of her salad.

"So, what's next?" Tara asked the whole table. "We have like, two hours until the finale right?"

"We haven't done the Fracker yet." Xophie tossed out her personal favorite. "And we all agreed to ride the Fracker this morning." Xophie reprimanded her friends like they had left it out intentionally.

"It was down Xophie, we couldn't ride it." Tara wasn't settling for random guilt. "But it's good now so, let's head over." Tara was now the 'go to' leader it seemed.

"If you don't mind, I'm just going to relax here for a little while." Mrs. Pruitt said, relieving all of them from the embarrassment of parental oversight. "I'll meet you at our usual place in the Wind Farm for the Finale?"

"See you then, Mom." Tara called out as she and the girls headed off to the Fracker.

"Meet at the Wind Farm at 7:30. Got it." Travis confirmed.

"And we are headed to the Gad About." Hank chimed in, daring Luci and Travis to disagree.

Luci smiled at that. It was definitely time to cool off. There were lockers to store their belts just around the corner. They grabbed a couple floats on the other side of the Cenote and hit the lazy river.

The Gad About led them through the gardens first, which was pretty amazing. They floated through ancient structures from around the world, everything from Angkor Wat, the Ziggurat, Egyptian pyramids, to both Mayan and Aztec ruins. There were Chinese temples and Peruvian terraced gardens along the slope of Mt. Alta. It was all thrown together like a Hollywood movie, but the colors and textures complemented each other and the effect was very relaxing. Luci noted how different the Egyptian pyramids were from Mayan and Aztec. The artwork depicted Gods of the dead, kings and headdresses, battles and travels to the underworld - all of it combined with lots of numbers.

Together they bobbed alongside a misty jungle of broad leafed plants, palms and flowering orchids. As they approached the Vonderheist, they could see the windmills and brick towers in the distance and the river took on a more forceful current. The water was choppy, especially when the Fracker flume came splashing down over them. By the time they passed the Sue Namee wave pool, an oasis of palms with its huge tidal waves, the floats were bouncing into one another and parkers were apologizing but laughing.

Circling behind the Centrifuge, they passed Greek and Roman sculptures carved into the surrounding buildings. Luci could identify some of the gods, there was Zeus, Hera, Athena… the detail was incredible. Lazy puffs of smoke trickled from Mt. Alta. You could spend days exploring just the art of Hoverpark!

Travis and Hank were such goofballs in the water. They were splashing each other and belly flopping onto the inner tubes. Even their way of relaxing was nerve wracking. Luci always liked a little time to herself so she let them drift off ahead of her. She didn't want to say anything, but Luci loved the lazy river. If she had the money (and a home) she would definitely build a lazy river of her own. Bobbing along in the ancient ruins she looked up towards the canopy and watched the shadows dance on the leaves. The sun was starting to dip and it shone in Luci's eyes but she lay back in her float and drifted off almost to sleep. With a bump, Hank interrupted her peace.

"Hey. Are you trying to sneak away from us?"

"I'm just taking a girl's moment." Luci smiled and Hank grabbed onto her tube to float. He started rocking the float.

"Stop it. Stop it Hank."

"I'm just kidding Luc."

"I'm relaxing here."

"OK, OK" Hank said and he settled into the flow of the river. Travis caught up with them just as they passed a family of six rafting together in a big crowded lump.

"You know, I've been thinking." Luci started as they enjoyed a bit of the river to themselves.

"Oh, crap." Hank mumbled and spun around in his float a little. Luci ignored him. It was a good place to talk; they were moving and going in and out of water spouts, so Luci continued.

"I've been thinking about the game master and his brother George." Luci announced. "I just don't feel right about it. You know - they looked almost identical, except the game master was wearing sandals. I don't remember if the guy who helped us this morning had on sandals or not. I just remember he was nice."

"He wasn't wearing sandals!" Hank knew that answer. "He was wearing dorky looking black shoes. I remember that."

"But the intruder had black shoes on." Travis said, jolted at his own memory.

"And that's the problem." Luci said looking at Travis. "It was the intruder who helped you out of the portal Travis. Not the game master."

Travis watched Luci carefully.

"It means the guy who helped us was also the intruder, the one who tried to stop the park." Luci said.

Travis was quiet for a moment but finally added. "Which makes the theory that he was chasing us and trying to harm the park harder to believe."

"What do you mean?" Hank said. "I thought we decided that the game master was the one who helped us?" He was getting confused.

"We did, but…" Travis tried to explain. "The game master is Winston. His brother George is the intruder who broke into the park today. He's the one we've been chasing around and he started the fire at the Fracker."

"Cy thought so. That's why George was arrested and put in holding." Luci added.

"The problem is, we think it was George who helped us today." Travis continued.

Hank paused nodding to himself. Then he added, "Honestly, I'm just glad you saw him. I kinda thought the guy who opened the panel was the ghost you know? The one Stan from the grab truck told me about, the engineer? I mean, he really looked the part." Hank was a bit shy to admit this, but he thought it was relevant and a little funny.

"Well that's ridiculous." Travis said, dismissing Hank's idea. "Since when do you believe in ghosts?"

"Well, duh! The name of the ghost is 'George' isn't it?" Hank defended himself. "It seems pretty obvious that George is not a ghost, but a real engineer. An engineer intruder it seems." He looked at both of them. Their eyes were wide and they were speechless, a true rarity.

"By George, you're right Hank! What was that story? I totally forgot about it." Luci was pretty excited about this new connection.

"I still don't see why a ghost story is going to tell us what is happening." Travis complained.

"Why wouldn't it, Travis?" Luci said. "Lots of truths are shared in stories."

"Hmmpf." Travis retorted.

"According to Stan," Hank started, "George was the engineer who died during construction. He's the one who takes the captain's wheel, the key hidden in the flotsam by the food truck. Stan told me about it which is how I got it today. Sometimes, George collects the key early in the morning before the guests get here."

"He collects the captain's wheel.?" Luci's eyes suddenly got big. "Travis, Hank, I think - I mean, if George?"

"George the ghost?"

"No, dufus, George the real engineer, the game master's twin brother. What if George has been regularly sneaking onto the ship?"

"You mean not just today? You think he's been sneaking onto the park on other days as well? But why would he do that? What would George be doing on the park?"

"I don't know, anything he wanted I guess?" Luci didn't have a good answer for that yet.

"I'm guessing he's not working on a toggle." Hank supposed.

"Really? I'm serious here Hank." Luci wasn't going to let it go.

"Maybe he has been planning for a while to destroy the park?" Travis added.

"Except the park is still here." Hank mumbled.

Luci was finding this intruder business more alarming now. It did seem like George had a plan. It seemed like he actually had some time to set everything up. And that was a very real concern.

"Since they caught George it's a moot point anyway right?" Travis asked aloud. "I mean, the park is fine."

"Maybe-" Luci said. It could also be a problem, she thought. "He surrendered pretty easily." And desperation is never that tidy and clean.

The Imag'n'ator

They got out of the Gad About at the Cenote by Amy's Lab and walked through the drying cave, coming out almost perfectly dry. Luci's hair was a bit tussled, but she wasn't one for primping so it didn't matter too much. Travis and Hank's hair managed to dry exactly the same, give or take some extra fluffiness.

"Now that there's time," Hank smiled, "Didn't you want to ride the Sail Train Luci?"

"Yes! Let's do it." Luci was pretty excited about the train. "I also want to do the Image'n'ator."

"That's a kiddie ride Luci." Travis was afraid someone would see them.

"I know, but I don't care. It seems really cool, and I'd like to see how our photos look in the ride."

"I'm game." Hank would ride with her. "We can take the train around to the Imag'n'ator."

With renewed energy and purpose the three of them practically ran to the sail train station in Bee Plaza. They were early and had to wait for a few minutes for the next train. Around them tired guests were relaxing in the shade. One young boy had a new toggle, already activated and he wore it with pride, fielding questions from other parkers. Travis and Hank complimented him on it and shared stories of their own toggles. It was obvious they were rock stars to the boy, especially Travis, who took the mantle of fame willingly. As they stood leaning against the railing, a steam whistle went off in the distance and Luci leaned out to watch the sail train coming into the station.

The train whistled again as it came barreling around the corner, its dusty white sails trimmed tight like a tall ship. Wind in the sails, it gained force coming around the curve. At the sight of the station, the crew pulled a large metal pinion and the sails suddenly luff, flapping loose in the air. The station crew opened the track at the switch slowing the train down as it gently docked at the station.

Luci's face beamed. It was the most amazing thing watching the train operate. The conductor called, "All Aboard" and together they boarded a window seat and settled into the car. With several loud clanks, they could feel the track switch back underneath them and then a gentle lifting of the right side of the car as the sails were trimmed and the train began moving. It was incredibly quiet, with the exception of the iron rails chattering below them as they glided along the track. Even in the car you could feel the tension between the track and the sails pulling the car slightly to the side.

Travis and Hank chatted together, people watching and sharing jokes, but Luci was all about the train. They remained onboard traveling to Shell Plaza station. The station was Victorian, with a huge clock and marble columns. It blended in well with the gardens of the Wrenaissance Theatre and the cobbled street leading up to the Imag'n'ator.

"We're here!" Luci jumped up, ready to go. On her teletab, she clicked one more experience off on her list. Ride a sail train, mission accomplished. It had been a fabulous day so far!

The Imag'n'ator was just to their immediate left. It was a time machine: a maze of gears, cogs and gauges all indicating the many measurements and fine tuning required for time travel. Hank, Luci and a reluctant Travis entered the line, wandering through a series of clockworks. A loud ticking is heard. The passage grew narrower and longer in appearance, finally reaching a brass and glass door that opened into a thick cypress swamp at night. They passed a 'cracker' shack, with the smell of bacon, swamp cabbage and smoke. A horse neighed in the background and a dog barked as they wind past a thatched chickee hut where a woman is sewing with a foot pedal machine. The path lead them down to an old rickety looking dock, and a series of John boats which the parkers board.

The boat ride through the swamp was dim and spooky in the palmettos and pines, but not too scary. As they floated along slowly, they pass wildlife animatronics like panthers and black bear, all set inside a jungle of native plants. The sun shone through the dirty glass ceiling and nurtured the mangrove swamp. Looking down into the water Luci thought she saw a mammoth grouper among the other fish swimming through the cypress knees.

Some of the animatronics are frightening, like rattlesnakes and a feral hog, but most of it was just wild and seems very serene. Without warning, the boat rocked twice, going over first one, then two, bumps and then it slipped into the open toothy smile of a huge alligator. In the dark tunnel of the gator's mouth, they hear 'scientists' adjusting the time.

"That's too far back, adjusting to MEEAD Center, prepare for re-launch"

Then, the boat dropped 30 ft. landing with a bold splash in the river. As their eyes adjusted to the light, Luci, Hank and Travis found themselves in a fantasy Hoverpark peppered with images from their own teletabs.

The boat ride took them around a mini Mt. Alta, as if they were on the Gad About. The Image'n'ator had a slightly elevated view of the park so they can see all the attractions. The images grew large in the dark around them, rising from their locations like a slide show.

"Hank, there you are on the Davinci flying machine!" Luci pointed out as the boat floated past the Vonderheist.

"And there's Travis and I flying through the wind farm on the Vonderheist - Travis did you take that picture?"

"No, that's a park camera shot."

"Who's that?" Luci was asking about a smiling staffer at a grab truck.

"That's Stan at the pizza stand." Hank said.

As the boat drifted past the Fracker, they saw the funny photos they took in the line.

"Look, Luci, you're a helpless victim - and now you've conquered the world!"

There were pictures of Ms. Pruitt at the Cenote Lounge, Tara and her friends, and a couple shots of Luci and Travis drinking Marvy. At the centrifuge there were several shots of Luci smiling with her hair glowing in the sun. And by Ma Ridgley's they saw some close ups of Travis grinning at them from the Gad About.

"Who took those? I didn't take those." Luci was a bit surprised by the sweet shots.

"I took them." Hank admitted fairly sheepish. 'They just kinda looked nice at the time."

"They are nice." Luci gave him a pat on the shoulder.

The ride was more fun than Travis thought. He got to relive the toggles and his roller coaster. They had park pictures of all three of them entering the park this morning, before all the intruder business, and there was even a shot of Luci with the little monkey that called her Mama. His favorite was the park shot of them riding the flume on the Fracker. The slide show ended with a musical flourish as the john boat docked at a fictional marina. In reality, the marina was a photo purchase hut, which you could line up and purchase photos. Hank jumped out of the boat and headed to the hut.

"I'm getting the photo package." Hank said shrugging as he stepped into the line.

"Seriously, Hank?" Luci couldn't believe it when she saw the prices. The photo package was enormously expensive.

"I told you I was getting it." Hank said defensively. "It's what I want."

"Ok, Ok." Luci couldn't imagine spending that kind of money on pictures but Hank was right. It was his money; he could spend it on what he wanted.

"So what have we got left to do? We only have a short time before we need to meet your Mom and Tara." She asked.

"We've done almost everything except the GENSys - and I'm not too keen on going back there." Travis looked at Luci to see how she'd take that information. Luci had really wanted to do the GENsys earlier in the morning.

"I agree!" Luci laughed. "There is no way I'm getting on one of those chairs today!"

28

Lessons

By the time Hank made his purchase, they had resigned themselves to swinging back by the Blue Hole to finish up their class assignments. Mostly, it was Travis who needed to finish his assignment but no one was pointing fingers. The Blue Hole was in Shell Plaza, right near the wind farm which is where the Pruitts liked to watch the Finale. Travis was dragging his feet. Even though he secretly liked the Blue Hole, he hated their assignment. Luci, Hank and Travis were walking past the formal gardens of the Wrenaissance Theatre when they heard the sudden sound of toggle music and the stone wall by the garden's gazebo start's glowing.

"Hear that? It's your teletab Travis!" Luci shouted. "No, wait, I think it's mine!!" Luci could hardly contain her excitement at the possibility to earn her first toggle.

"Wait, I think it's mine!" Hank reached for his teletab and together they realized *all* of their teletabs were playing music, meaning the glowing stone wall in front of them was for who exactly?

"Have you ever had this happen to you Travis?" Hank asked, still a bit confused.

"No, I'm not sure what this means." Travis was a little anxious, he really wanted this last toggle and if his teletab was playing, it might be his last chance today.

"My teletab is showing all of us are supposed to go for this toggle?" Hank said, still confused.

"Maybe it is all of us." Luci chimed in. "Maybe it's a team toggle?"

"That's ridiculous. Why would there by a team toggle? It doesn't make sense." Travis couldn't help being rude. He was supposed to be the expert at toggles.

"He's right." Hank shrugged. "There aren't any 'team' toggles - at least that we know of?"

The portal was definitely open and all their teletabs were glowing so the three of them stepped up to the doorway, arguing the whole time. The argument stopped when they saw keys from all of their teletabs light up on the screen. There was Luci's wing, Hank's captain's wheel and Travis's pedals. They started moving parts around. It was chaos at first, because they all worked at the same time. Travis tried to take over, but Luci just ignored him and even backed into him a little to nudge him off her section of screen. In a short amount of time, she had her wing attached to a drive bar, the wings even doubled on the screen. Travis managed to push his way past and soon his pedals were linked up to the same drive bar for the wings. A few more cogs manipulated by Travis and Luci at turns, activated the pedals. Hank who'd been standing back, watching them, suddenly stepped in to attach his helm to the drive bar. Before they knew it, together they had created a flying machine - it was fabulous! The blue print screen glows in recognition, breaks out into celebration, and the three of them jump up and down in a raucous cheer.

"We did it!"

"I told you it was a team toggle."

"It has to be the first! I've never even heard of this happening before!"

The toggle began printing, and their laughter slowed down little by little as worry began setting in. They began looking at each other in silence. Who would get this toggle?

Travis, embarrassed by what was obviously greed, really wanted it, it would be his seventh and he needed it to finish the challenge and get into the Cave for real. He could tell by Luci's face however, she wanted it badly - and Luci is the only one without a toggle at all for crying out loud! Travis felt guilty. Luci was anxious and almost gave him the stink eye when, much to their surprise, the tray moved over and the printer started laying out another toggle. Hank released an audible sigh of relief. He figured, he would be last on the list, knowing the facts and all, so he wasn't going to make a large claim. He was just grateful. Happy and grateful. They were all getting toggles!

"It is beautiful." Luci said mesmerized. "I can't wait to activate it."

"There's a gift shop at the Wrenaissance. Come on, it's just a little bit further." Travis said.

At the gift shop, Luci, Hank and Travis went to the register to activate their toggles immediately. It was fantastic, with all the parts spinning and the little wings flying, Luci was mesmerized. Travis and Hank each had two to activate and they shared Luci's excitement.

Travis was slightly disappointed no one handed him an extra key or ticket to get into the Cave? In fact, it appeared this toggle didn't work that way. Perhaps it didn't count towards the seven? Or maybe that wasn't up to the staffers in the gift shop? There was no acknowledgement of getting into the Cave in the foreseeable future. And the day was almost over. It was problematic, but Travis would live. He'd had a great day considering and it was probably best not to ask.

Travis and Hank were playing with some of the toys in the shop but Luci didn't have any extra money to spend. The activation fee tapped her out and honestly, she hated shopping.

"Look, I'm going outside. I'll meet you in the gardens, OK?" She said.

"Sure Luc. We'll be right there." Travis and Hank replied. They were busy building robotic arms.

Outside, Luci found a bench by the fountain where she sat and admired her toggle glowing and spinning in the twilight. She didn't have a belt, so she just toggled it onto the buttonhole of her jeans like a belt buckle. It wasn't perfect, but it worked. Luci was not sure how they achieved a team toggle, but she was pleased about it. Who wouldn't be? Travis and Hank were her best friends ever and today was perhaps the highlight of her life. The Hoverpark wasn't so bad. She could see how the park promoted conservation, and for the first time it didn't feel quite so bad being a recipient of the Hoverpark Community Scholarship Fund. Right here, right now, Luci could get into this whole 'Live the Wonder' thing. She certainly understood why Travis and Hank loved it so much.

All around her, the sun was starting to set and it painted the sky a startling red and purple. Puffs of maroon clouds hung in the red sky, as the sun shone brilliantly orange and dipped slowly, slowly further down leaving the sky dark purple above it.

"Red sky at night, Sailor's delight" Luci said out loud. It meant tomorrow was going to be another beautiful day. Of course, a brilliant sunset like that also meant there was a lot of pollution in the air. The particulates make the sky extra colorful.

In the waning hue of the sunset, Luci thought she saw a ring neck garter snake slip under a rock beside her and she leaned over to investigate. Hiding in the shadows of the palmettos were young fish in the pond! Looking closer she noticed a frog's eyes poking up from under a clump of grass and a blue heron was hunting around the other side of the rock. It was incredible that she had missed these details earlier!

Luci got up and wandered around the back of the waterfall to explore the next pool over and surprisingly found an alligator with babies reposing on the fountain side of the pool. That is definitely not supposed to happen here, of that she was sure! What the heck was going on?

Suddenly from behind her, Luci heard a footstep and she spun around to find herself face to face with one of the twins. Slowly she backed against the rocks facing him, preparing to defend herself. Luci's heart was pounding. She glanced down at his shoes to figure out who it was, then seeing the sandals, she paused. It was the game master.

"So, the game master walks the park. Big deal." She said, remembering Hank's statement earlier. She tried to remain calm.

"Yes, the game master walks the park." He smiled and relaxed his stance a little.

"Nice shirt." He added.

Luci's face scrunched, puzzled and then she remembered she was wearing her Rhino Love shirt.

"I used to work with 'Save the Rhinos.'

"How'd that work out?" Luci sassed back. She was not comfortable with adults and she was still unsure about the game master.

"Not well. Obviously," He continued. "But it was pretty much a losing battle from the start. That's why we built the HoverArk you know. Just think of it. Most of the world is wallowing in poverty, whole jungles have been cut down, and wildlife species are going extinct by the hundreds. In the midst of all this destruction, we make this incredible discovery - we can create floating islands of refuge! The Gulf of Mexico dies but we've created a floating Utopia, a research station that can help heal the earth. It is literally an Ark of all the greatest technology, art, inventions, architecture and green energy solutions. The HoverArk was a sign of hope, a promise for the future!

Without dropping her eyes, Luci responded, "But it's not. It's a theme park."

His face fell and she almost regretted it. It was a thing with her, this pushing of buttons.

"You are correct Luci. It's a theme park. But that is not the design, it is what happened. When the state of Florida allowed the University to sell it to Hoverparks Inc., C.A.H.P...."

"Citizens against Hoverpark." Luci interjected.

"Yes – exactly - C.A.H.P. tried to save the Ark. We took it all the way to the Federal Supreme Court, arguing that projects created with public money should remain the property of the American people - but the Court insisted the grant contract did not establish public rights."

"Of course they did. I mean, did you honestly think you'd win?" Luci asked.

"Yes." He looked at her defensively. "It was outrageous. This project belonged to everyone, all of humanity. And what did they do? They stole our best chance for saving the world and made it a theme park of all things! What kind of a joke is that?"

"At least it's a theme park where parkers are helping 'scientists' save the world." Luci couldn't help laughing a little. She laughed when she was nervous. And she was a little embarrassed since honestly; she'd just bought into the park not two minutes before.

"See. You get it." He continued. "They took the real thing and made it a game. It was part of the plan actually. They called the parks a new education model - and used teachers to help them develop it. It was how they gained community support. They also said it would create jobs. Jobs! What kind of jobs are these? Do you want to be a professional pizza pusher? We were offering real world solutions and they choose profits and minimum wage jobs instead…."

"It is what it is." Luci said quietly. "There's nothing you can do about it."

"Maybe. But sometimes things are not as they seem." he smiled. "The battle for Hoverpark isn't over."

"What is that supposed to mean?" Luci thought. The battle for Hoverpark was over a long time ago, but all her fears bubbled up again.

"You needn't worry too much; you won't learn about it in history class." He laughed and slipped back into the bushes. She heard him chuckling even after she lost sight of him, then she heard the boys calling her name.

"Luci? Luci?"

"Over here," she answered loudly.

Travis and Hank come running around the corner to show her their purchases. Travis had bought some chocolate bugs that had hearts and organs that glowed in the dark. Hank had a solar leaf pin that charged his toggles in the dark and he held up a bright new toggle belt.

"We got you something." They grinned at her presenting her with the belt. She took the belt tearfully, and held it, a bit overwhelmed at the generosity of her friends.

"What's wrong Luci?"

"Nothing." Luci smiled. "Nothing's wrong at all." She was so proud of her belt; she put it on and attached her toggle immediately.

"What were you doing all the way over here?"

"Yes. That is a good question. I was following some wildlife I noticed - which is weird enough - and you know what Hank? The game master does walk the park! He came up as I was watching those baby alligators. We had a little chat."

"Baby alligators?" Travis was confused, but looked in the direction of Luci's point and there they were. At least there were their eyes, small pairs of them, glowing in the bushes on the other side of the fountain.

"Got it!" Hank snapped another image with his teletab and linked it up on his assignment.

"So, what did you talk to the game master about?"

"The history of the park mostly, he's actually a pretty bitter guy. He said something funny. He said the battle for the Hoverpark wasn't over yet. What do you think that means?"

"Don't know - but our day is almost over, so it will have to happen soon if we're going to see it." Travis said laughing. He was in a good mood.

"Come on. Let's go. We're supposed to meet Mom at the Wind Farm. Are you ready?"

"Yeah. He did say we won't be reading about it in history class." Luci added.

"Will we be able to collect it for our class assignment?" Hank asked laughing and gave Travis a little shove.

"I have my assignment done." Travis announced indignantly.

"Barely."

Travis gave him a dirty look. He didn't actually have his assignment done. He was going to collect a wind turbine in the wind farm as well.

"I still have some money on my account; I thought I'd get an ice cream on the way?" Hank added as his friends shook their heads.

29

Finale

As they wove through the remaining crowds into the wind farm, Travis used his teletab to locate his mother. They found her with Tara, Xophie and Monica. They had a great spot, on a bench just under a windmill.

The way the Finale is designed, anywhere you stand in the park is special. Parkers watching in Bee Plaza for instance can see the world glowing on the dome of the GENsys. The Pruitts liked the wind farm near the Vonderheist where they could see both the edge of the GENsys and the Centrifuge. Also, the wind farm gave them a direct view of the Fracker which plays a big part of the Finale story.

Shortly after the sky grew dark, the park began transforming and the Finale slowly started building. The rides officially closed at sunset when an interactive lightshow officially began. Like stars appearing on the horizon, lights along the buildings and on cables draped over Mt. Alta activated at dusk and flickered in synchronicity with the music. Guests gathered all along the park plazas, filled benches and stood along garden walls to watch the evening show. It was a slow transition. First lights, then images wound around the park. The darker it got, the greater the coordination of all the lights.

Relaxing on the bench, Hank watched vendors begin weaving through the crowd with hot chocolate, wine, Marvy and cups of corn. As the music grew with a rising crescendo, spotlights swirled around the park in wild colors and then suddenly, with the final beat of the timpani drum, there was total darkness. Luci actually grabbed Hank's arm in fear. A few young people screamed, and some babies began crying but the darkness was short lived. It was the dramatic introduction to the formal show, the infamous Finale.

Once their eyes adjusted to the stars, a rising fog from the river created a smoke screen across the park. Projected on the smoke was a looming cityscape, beautiful with twinkling lights in the windows that echoed the stars. A loud cacophony of noises grew with the shadows; horns honking, sirens, music fading in and out, and an occasional shout. It was the sounds of a city, the noise of the world around them.

Below the city sounds, there was the slow rise of an orchestra and sparks began flying from the fog. As the orchestra grew louder, the Gad About River gurgled and churned. A flash of pyrotechnics highlighted the Hoverpark's actual buildings, which slowly 'rose' from the mist, replacing the crumbling cityscape. It was glorious in the lights, first the ancient structures are revealed in the mist and then the labs with indoor lights glowing.

The story was the legend of the MEEAD Center, starting with the labs and buildings as they were before the volcano disrupted the island. They could see activity inside the buildings. With excitement, they recognized the tesla coils sparking inside Vonderheist's lab. They saw Dr. Wren floating a ball in his lab and the spinning stars of the GENsys.

The image of a working MEEAD center remained just a moment, then pulsing lights and a crescendo in the music accompanied fireworks sparking along the river. Guests looked at their feet as a low rumbling began below them. The sound of drums grew in urgency, and then Fracker cracked through the side of the volcano. The water glowed red like lava, and one flume dove down giving parkers a brief glimpse of the shadow of Dr. Vonderheist escaping the fire.

In a flash of lights and gushing water spouts, the fog dissipated to reveal the smoking peak of Mt. Alta and a full on fireworks display began. Explosive fireworks rose over the volcano into the night sky and the fountains in the plazas and on Mt. Alta came alive! The colors went from fiery yellow, orange, and reds then changed to white with blues and greens. Climbing along the rocks, vines began covering the volcano and blooming with the existing the vegetation. The Gad About River was alive with spouts of water glistening in the light and the park seemed to move ever so slightly to imitate the rise of hovering.

As Mt. Alta grew in green glory, a world of animals, many extinct, began emerging in lights among the plants. Sparks of technology bring well being to the island - water flowed along aqua ducts, into hanging gardens, and fish swam in the fountains. Manatees lounged in the Gad About as the river feds fields of corn through an intricate canal system.

The island is presented in all its glory, as a utopia of plants and animals, ancient buildings, modern technology and the power of full human potential. Luci realized with a touch of surprise it was the creation of HoverArk. The sky blazed with twirling toggles that shone over the rides which sparkled in their lighted glory.

Standing in the open, parkers watched glowing planes swoop through the wind farm. The Centrifuge rose and 'floated' in full color. The GENsys glowed like the world. Everywhere was the best seat in the house for this light show. The last fireworks rose over Mt. Alta, when the music came to a close, with sparks of light falling through the sky, tumbling back to earth. The park was glorious in its night lights and the smoke from the fireworks settled like clouds above the dead gulf below them.

It was time to leave the Hoverpark. In the dim night lighting, the ground on the park began glowing, thousands of lights in different colors and flowing images indicating the exits. As reluctant as they all were, they were tired. Ms. Edison was expecting them at Shell Bay so they gathered together and started following the white lit shells glowing on the pavement, working their way with the crowd to the balloon docks.

"Look a bee" Xophie said, pointing to an image on the ground.

"We're following the shells" Hank reminded her.

Some parkers liked to hurry and make the first balloons off the island, but the Pruitts tended to enjoy the dark and quiet of the park on the way out, casually chatting with each other and admiring the whole appearance of giant balloons rising and falling. Once you get behind, you might as well just relax and wait. Penelope, Tara, Travis, Hank, Xophie, Monica and Luci filed into the back of the line for the balloons. They could make out some members of the rest of their class in front of them. At the base of the ship were gathering docks where families and school groups could reconnect at the end of the day. They were headed to Shell Bay, where they met this morning.

Incredibly, beside them was the same Mother and child they rode up with that morning. This time, the child had his sun goggles on his head and he was fast asleep in his Mother's arms, leaning against her shoulder.

Luci smiled at her, 'Did he have fun?"

"We both did." She answered. "He fell asleep after the fireworks, he's so tuckered out!"

The line passed through the garden in stop and go fashion, which was to be expected as they filled the gondolas. Some parkers sat on the rock wall as they waited. Luci stepped around to the side into the shadows and was admiring a natural fountain with a waterfall trickling into the pool. In the dark, she could make out bits of glimmering around the waterfall where the water was churning ever so slightly into the pond.

"Look Travis!" Luci called out to Travis who moved into the dark with her, "Look, I think it's alive - it looks like tiny sea walnuts!"

"You're right Luci." Since when did the Hoverpark have bio luminous animals? Travis was perplexed. How did they do that? And why?

"Mom" He called Penelope Pruitt. She studied biology, she would know these things for sure.

"Did you see this?" Travis pointed out the sea walnuts.

"No and wow." Mrs. Pruitt was looking around in the rocks by the waterfall. "The park must have been enhanced with a system to make some of the water features aquariums."

"Those systems always existed actually," said a voice quietly by their shoulder, startling Mrs. Pruitt. Much to the surprise of Luci and Travis, beside Mrs. Pruitt stood George, the 'ghost' engineer. It was definitely him. Luci was shocked. The intruder was not arrested. In fact, he was very much free and wandering the park.

"It looks like the game master's brother wanders the park too." Luci said quietly to Travis. And that was terrifying!

30

Path of Egress

THE INTRUDER STEPPED UP NEXT to them, so close you could smell him, which was a tad gross. He smelled like dirt and lightly of fresh fish.

"The aquarium system always existed but it has just recently been activated - finally put to use."

Luci and Travis found themselves hiding slightly behind Penelope Pruitt. What was George doing here? Didn't Winston call the police?

Mrs. Pruitt was completely oblivious to the danger. "What is the purpose though? These fountains are so close to the public. Sea Walnuts aren't like goldfish. People will end up killing them out of curiosity."

"That is an excellent point, Ms. Pruitt. And I can tell you when we designed the island, there wasn't supposed to be a public."

There was a brief silence as Penelope Pruitt took in the information just given to her. First, he was one of the original engineers - which was pretty exciting - but he also knew her name. While it was easy for security to read parker teletabs, it was a bit creepy for this strange man to know her. Finally Mrs. Pruitt noticed Luci and Travis quietly behind her trying to pull her back, away from the man and into the lighted path. The intruder also realized this and quickly reached out his hand in introduction.

"Winston. My name is Winston. And I am the game master for Hoverpark." He smiled. "At least I was, until just recently."

"Mom, he's lying." Travis couldn't contain himself. "His name is George and he's been banned from the park since it opened. He broke onto the park this morning and we've been following him all day. Mom, he's the intruder." With that said, Travis stood tall and brave next to his Mom.

"Well, you have it half right, but please speak quietly Travis. You're in no danger. I assure you. I'm also the one who helped you escape from the portal earlier."

"Why did you do that?" Luci asked suddenly jumping into the conversation. Travis looked on quietly. He was cautious, but it didn't hurt to find out the truth. He noticed that his Mom had not relaxed.

"Please just hear me out," the intruder said. "There's a little more to it than it seems. Yes, I did have to break onto the park today, so I guess in that respect I am the 'intruder' so to speak, but I am also the one and only game master." He paused before adding, "At least I was until last week."

Travis looked over at Luci to see how she was responding. Luci was always a good thermometer for lying adults. She was wearing her angry girl look, but she was listening.

Winston paused briefly to watch them nod and then continued uninterrupted. "My name is Winston. Months ago George, the *real* George, snuck onto the park and hacked my biotag. We use them for staffing here as well. I didn't know he'd bypassed security. I didn't even know he was on the ship, but I left the last week to visit a friend and when I returned I couldn't get back on. My clearance was gone, and the bioscans wouldn't let me pass the entrance gates. I tried to contact security, but George had taken over as game master, as me really, and they didn't know something was wrong. I lost all access to my bio account; everything - George had complete control. He has been planning this for years it seems."

Winston paused again to see how the story was being received.

Travis made a little huff, but Luci placed her hand on his shoulder and whispered quietly, "It makes sense Travis. Think about it, remember, he had a special code to open your portal, he must be an insider."

"It took some doing, but you saw how I got back on." Winston continued. "And Mrs. Pruitt, I do apologize for that ruckus. It couldn't be helped."

Penelope Pruitt was quiet. She was entering the story a little late, but learned early in life that listening was the best method of getting to the truth of the matter.

"Who was that woman?" Luci blurted out. Luci wasn't always patient.

A big smile crossed Winston's face, "That was Amy, the real Amy. She still lives in the University of South Florida area; she works as a waitress believe it or not. I didn't have any other contacts left outside of the ship. Spending all your days inside the ship on a computer can make you a bit of a recluse- and I didn't know who I could trust. So I went back to Amy to see if she could help me. You know, that's one of the reasons George and I had a falling out. We both had a huge crush on Amy. She chose me over George. He never forgave me for that." Winston looked down and shrugged. "And I don't think he realizes that was her yet."

From the light, an impatient Hank came running up with Tara, Xophie and Monica clumped behind him giggling over pictures on their teletab.

"What's up guys?" Hank asked.

"Oh, hey…" Hank recognized Winston as the man who helped them free Travis earlier today. "Thanks for today. You ran off so fast" Hank looked around at the others who were not wearing their happy faces.

"You're welcome." Winston smiled genuinely.

"What's happening?" Hank asked. He could read the tension.

"Hank," Travis started. "This is the intruder - but according to him not really, I mean he is but he says he isn't the real intruder." Travis paused.

"But...?" Hank was confused and he looked around at everyone else. Winston took over.

"I am Winston, the game master of Hoverpark." And he held out his hand for Hank to shake.

Hank shrugged. "I told you," he said to Travis and shook Winston's hand.

Winston continued. He didn't have much time. "So it was pretty upsetting. George has been masquerading as me and serving as the game master for almost a week. He did a great job eliminating me. I had to create that crazy distraction to get back on the ship."

Luci jumped in. "People could have gotten hurt you know. With the power out, and the lack of communications, we thought you were going to blow up the park or something."

"Blow up the park!" Hank was shocked. That was the first he'd heard of that. He looked at Travis who shrugged. Luci could be so dramatic.

"Or something..." Luci clarified looking quickly at Hank and Travis. Her fears weren't part of this right now. That whole brownout business was really scary.

"Whoa," Winston was a little shocked at the Luci's accusation. "I only set the breaker box on fire, up by the Fracker! I was trying to get through a portal. I didn't create the brownout - that was George. You can't do that kind of damage with one breaker box here."

Luci looked at him suspiciously. Why would the other twin cut the power?

And you're right, what he did was frightening. He admits it. I'm pretty sure it scared him actually. He didn't really know what would happen when he flipped the power off." Winston said, almost to himself.

"Why would 'George' disrupt the park like that?" Luci asked.

"Well, partially to stop me." Winston laughed. "He figured out I was on board the ship."

Winston suddenly became very serious, and secretive. "But I was actually just interrupting George's big plan. He was in the process of something incredible. And now - well, he's succeeded. He's succeeded! We're really going to do it! Together, the -"

"*Together*?!" Luci interrupted. "Are you mad?" Luci was not taking the twin unity switch lightly. "He stole your identity, he attacked you and had you jailed."

"He also freed me you know. Yes, at first I was furious. Who wouldn't be? But once we talked and I learned the big picture. He's quite amazing. My brother, Luci, for all his shortcomings, is the true idealist. We were a constant team growing up, but George was my conscience. He always did the right thing. I was the coward. When we were students, I was the one who sold out to Hoverpark. I sold him out too you know. But George, well - George is the one who always truly believed." Winston paused and looked around to see how they were taking the story.

"I know it was frightening, but George is right. I've known that for a long time now, but I was too afraid to do something about it. George on the other hand - remember the reboot?"

They all nodded. Who could forget the reboot?

"The reboot was the last step in George's plan and that's what I'm here to tell you." Winston smiled a little and opened his hands wide. "George and I would like to announce the return of HoverArk."

31

Luminous

Travis' mouth dropped. Penelope stepped back up front, recognizing the implications of Winston's words.

"The HoverArk no longer exists Mr. Winston." Penelope Pruitt said very decidedly.

"Oh, but it absolutely does. May I call you Penelope? It's all right here; everything as it was first designed, it has been here all along." Winston made a grand gesture out towards the stars along the horizon.

As Penelope Pruitt's face grew darker, Winston added. "There's nothing you can do, the decision is made and the transition will happen very safely. No one will be hurt."

There was a heavy pause. The air itself almost crackled from the electricity in their brains as the synapses snapped with the possibility. Penelope Pruitt looked over at the sea walnuts and turned to Hank and Tara who were watching them closely.

"Hank, would you and Tara please have Xophie and Monica get in line for the hot air balloon?" She gave him no room for argument. "Tell them we need to wait for the last transport balloon and we'll be with them shortly."

"How do you know no one will be hurt? It's seems obvious George created a lot of trouble for everyone, yourself included. If he was responsible for that brownout, it was reckless. How can you trust him? Why are you letting him do this?" Penelope Pruitt looked approvingly at Luci.

"That's a good question. First, he's my brother and I know him. George is brilliant and committed. His plan is a good one, though somewhat poorly executed today. As I said, he was rushed into that by me. George isn't a terrorist, he builds solutions. And this I assure you is a grand solution."

Winston continued, "And secondly, honestly, it's tough being in this cave. It may sound all romantic and fun, but the truth is I've been stuck inside that office for almost 8 years. I'm ready to get my life back. I miss that sense of purpose, living with a true vision." He paused for a moment.

"Don't you?" Winston added, watching Penelope Pruitt.

Penelope Pruitt was shocked at his intimacy.

"You don't know me or what I miss or want." She practically spat back at him.

"I don't. But I thought perhaps – well, things are just getting worse down there. It's scary really. I found that out this week. I thought I had abandoned everything for the park, but the truth is we've all been abandoned. Parkers are being entertained into acceptance. You're sold an experience that says you're helping to save the world, but you're just playing a game. Students are taught trivia, not knowledge; and every dollar you earn comes with a scheme to get it back."

Winston could tell he'd hit a nerve. "But back to the HoverArk. There is nothing you can do to stop it, even if you wanted to." He looked at Penelope Pruitt. "It's too late for that, but -"

After a brief pause, Winston tried the big pitch. "How would you like to help us throw off the mantle of corporate greed and profit?"

Travis whispered to Luci, "What's a mantle?"

"It's like a cloak." She whispered back.

Penelope Pruitt stood silent.

Winston continued, "George has uploaded the last of the programs. The reboot is complete. We have no choice, we are returning to the original design of HoverArk tonight."

"What about all these people?" Ms. Pruitt asked. "What is your grand plan for all the people on the ship?"

"The parkers are leaving. The park staffers go ashore this evening on furlough. The dedicated few will stay on and we will be returning this ship to the task of working for the common good. We set sail shortly after the park closes. You can say goodbye forever to the Hoverpark."

There was an ominous silence, and some confusion. A wave of disappointment overwhelmed Travis. All he'd heard was 'Goodbye forever to the Hoverpark." He'd never finish the game. He would not get a chance to go into the cave properly, as an accomplished toggler. Hoverpark would be gone. All he worked for… his heart was slowly being crushed. Winston looked over them again, taking measure.

He looked at Penelope Pruitt and asked directly, "You could join us? We can use another veterinarian and a group of creative, smart, young people. Or you can simply go back to your life. It's up to you. You have a choice, but it must be made now." Winston said.

Winston had a broad grin on his face. Travis realized Winston was exuberant and it was a little scary. Travis had never known an adult to act that way. He glanced over at Luci to see how she was responding.

"So, why did you choose us?" Luci asked Winston.

"Several reasons, not the least of which is, you've proven yourself. Haven't you realized that? Take that toggle you're wearing for instance," Winston pointed to the flying machine.

"I created that puzzle years ago. It's one of the most important ones. And it's never been solved before."

"But it's just a flying machine?" Luci thought the hardest puzzles would be the most obscure.

"Yes, but this is the toggle that you can't collect on your own. It takes teamwork. If you have a wing, you will not be able to collect the helm or the pedal gear."

"So it was just random?"

"No Luci. It was not random. It was teamwork. True success is only achieved through teamwork. How else can we move forward? People need to work together if we are going to have a tolerable future."

Travis was listening but not hearing Winston's words. He was thinking through his options. What would it be like without the Hoverpark? How could he save this situation? He didn't actually have to say goodbye.

A lightening started blooming inside Travis. If they stayed, he would not have to hand in his assignment! He wouldn't have to finish any homework in fact, because he wouldn't be going back to school. Travis was slowly but surely grabbing this opportunity and all its potential. He could do this! Beside him, Luci was brimming with excitement. Hank was very quiet, but Travis knew he would join them if Travis asked him to. He looked at Tara and his Mom to see how they were responding, Tara was watching her Mom carefully. For a minute Travis thought it was a go, but his heart dropped as Mrs. Pruitt responded.

"That is ridiculous. We can't just drop our lives and join this ship."

"It is not as ridiculous as you might think, Penny. You would not be the first Pruitt to do so."

She looked at him suspiciously. That was out of line, a ploy to entice her to stay. Before she got a chance to respond however, Winston looked alarmingly at his park badge and made to move.

"Now if you'll excuse me, I've got a lot of work to do, and a very short time to do it in." Winston smiled back at them and started to step back into the shadows…just as Officer Cy Pinter stepped out of them!

32

GOODBYE

"WHAT IS GOING ON HERE?" Cy stopped and surveyed their circle, but by the time he turned around Winston was gone.

He started to head after him but stopped and pointed accusingly at Luci and Travis.

"You two, I told you I would block you from the Hoverpark and I will." Cy snarled. He faced them with authority.

"You are hereby banned from the park. You will leave today and do not try to reenter."

Afterwards, Cy turned his back on them and bolted into the dark.

"Hmmfff." Luci huffed, arms across her chest.

Travis was too focused on his Mom and her decision to even respond. Penelope looked at the two of them. She wasn't going to get worked up about Cy right now. They had much more important things to talk about.

"I'm in." Luci said suddenly. Her eyes lit up, and she stood tall at the announcement."

"Luci? What are you doing?" Travis was not comfortable with this turn of events. What if Luci gets to stay and he doesn't?

"I'm in Travis. I'm staying." Luci looked at him. "It's OK. I don't have much to lose really and think about it - the HoverArk!"

Travis was scared. She was joining George! The scary twin who tried to chase them down, tried to trap him in a portal and shut down the park!

"You are going to stay on this ship with George?" He asked. And without us, he thought.

"George isn't so bad. He lacks some social graces, but he seemed like a good guy." Lucy said. Luci realized when she met George, she'd actually liked him. Now that she understood the reboot, she liked him better.

She added. "George is OK, Travis." Travis wasn't entirely convinced.

"Luci, you are such an excellent student. You have a lot of promise, are you sure you want to give it all up? You'll be an elementary school dropout you know?" Penelope Pruitt addressed Luci candidly.

"I thought about that Ms. Pruitt. But I don't think I'm going to miss much." Luci smiled," Though, I am concerned that I haven't learned about all the presidential pets yet."

Ms. Pruitt chuckled at that. Luc was one of the brightest kids she knew.

"But Luci, you don't know anyone on this ship." It was frightening.

"I know. But I've gone through many foster families Ms. Pruitt." Luci looked at her and shrugged.

"And I know you?" Luci smiled with the question. Would she? That would make her decision easier.

Penelope Pruitt took a deep breath. At her side, Travis looked longingly at his Mom. He couldn't imagine Luci getting to stay and him leaving.

"Please," he begged. But Ms. Pruitt ignored him and turned to Tara.

"Tara?" She asked.

"I think we should do it" Tara announced.

Travis and Luci were shocked, but Tara had a confident air about her. "I really want to, Mom. This place is filled with information - more than I ever imagined. There's so much to learn here and can you imagine being able to relax in the Gad About whenever you wanted?"

"You don't know about that Tara. What are you going to do about your friends?" Penelope asked.

"Luci will be here. She's my friend." Tara looked at Luci. "Aren't you?"

"Of course!" Luci put her arm around Tara glad to have a companion. "Best buds forever."

Penelope paused, thinking it through. Grinning she looked around at them all. What did they really have to lose? What an adventure; imagine the kids living on the HoverArk! And it was an opportunity. It would be more than she could ever give them at home, struggling all the time just to make ends meet. If it didn't work out...well, she'd think about that later. Sometimes you have to make a leap of faith.

"Well alright then." Penelope said, smiling with a certain resolve. "We'll do it."

There was a loud cheer! They couldn't believe it actually - were they really going to stay here on the Hoverpark and call it home? Travis couldn't help but wonder why his mother would make such a bold decision. It wasn't like they had a lot to go back to, just a leaky roof and bills. But still?

"Hank, what about you?" Travis looked over at Hank, while Luci nodded excitedly.

"I'm going to go with Xophie and Monica back to the parking deck." Hank said, and everyone stopped in disbelief.

"But Hank?" Travis started to ask.

"Hank has his family Travis," Penelope Pruitt started to say, but she was interrupted by Hank.

"I can't. I just can't." Hank looked down. "I haven't told any of you, but I have - there are -" Hank was nervous but he had to say it out loud.

"I'm sick Travis," He said apologetically, "I can't go. I have doctors that I need to see. I don't have a choice really."

There was total silence as everyone took this information in.

"So that's why -" Luci suddenly had tears in her eyes. They had all taken Hank's scan at the Vonderheist lightly, she thought he had just been scared but - Luci was silently crushed in the dark and she refused to look him in the eye.

It was Penelope Pruitt who first reached out and gave Hank a big hug.

"Honey, why didn't you tell us?"

"It doesn't matter. There's nothing you can do. I've had the best day ever though." Hank was trying to be positive. He was looking at Travis, waiting for Travis to say or do something.

"What am I going to do without you?" Travis was suddenly not as confident.

"You'll get by." Hank gently punched Travis in the shoulder. He knew it was his loss really. This field trip was sort of a last hurrah before the treatments began.

"Once you get better, you can join us, OK?" Travis didn't know that could actually happen, but he was not good at letting go. He stood there frozen in place. Not moving, not even blinking.

"Yes. That's a good plan." Hank hesitated and looked over at the line to the balloon basket loading up. Xophie and Monica were waving at them to hurry.

"Well, it looks like they're loading the last of the parkers, so I'd better shove off."

"Hank?" Travis didn't know what to do, so he reached out his hand, but Hank gave him a hug instead.

"It's Ok Travis." Hank looked down. "I'll catch up with you."

Luci suddenly came from behind, and embraced him in a big hug. "I'll write. You'll have to find me, and I won't mention you by name so you'll be safe, but I'll write."

Hank wasn't sure what that meant either, but he nodded. "I'll look for it Luci, I will."

With a last look, Luci clasped Hank's hand and held it to his toggle. Hank nodded, though he didn't know why.

The line for Shell Dock was growing smaller and they could see the balloon conductor motioning for Xophie and Monica to get into the gondola.

"I need to go board now." Hank turned his head trying to break away. He didn't want them to see him cry.

"Don't forget us." Luci said and impulsively she kissed Hank on the cheek. Travis's mouth dropped in shock and Luci turned beet red as she stepped away and let Hank go.

33

Going Home

Flustered, Hank ran toward Xophie and Monica, talking to the two of them as all three reluctantly got into the basket. The conductor latched the door behind them, and Hank turned around and feebly waved at Travis, Tara, Luci and Mrs. Pruitt, still shadows at the edge of the tree line. He couldn't even see them wave back.

"I'll never forget." Hank whispered and his balloon lifted off the dock. The gondola was filled with sweaty, tired parkers that swayed with the motion of the balloon as it gently floated back to earth on its tether. Monica and Xophie were angry, refusing to believe that Hank didn't know why the Pruitts were not on their balloon. They decided to give him the silent treatment, which suited him as well. In the dark, under the stars, Hank couldn't help thinking how amazingly beautiful the balloons were, glowing as they drift down to earth.

When Hank, Xophie and Monica landed, they were within three feet of Shell Bay, where the rest of their classmates were waiting. Ms. Edison was checking off the last of her geotagged students and coordinating with the other teachers to be sure they had the complete roster. She anxiously checked her watch, they were supposed to leave five minutes ago but there were still several children missing.

"Hank. Travis - Travis Pruitt?" Ms. Edison made eye contact with Hank and then looked about distractedly for Travis. In frustration, she grabbed Hank's attention.

"Hank, where is Travis?" She was stepping up just as her teletab alarm started ringing.

"What is going on?" It was obvious Ms. Edison was talking with several of the other teachers. A whole group of the 5th grade was missing.

"Hank. I need you over here right now."

"Yes, Ms. Edison." Hank resigned himself to the task at hand. The busses were pulling up to the bay, students were beginning to board but Hank's presence was requested by the panicking teachers and chaperones gathered at just by the exit.

Before they could ask their questions however, the Hoverpark suddenly lit up and the air around them started buzzing. Everyone on the ground looked up at the glowing lights and were mesmerized as the ship slowly started lifting into the air. Several of the staffers, carrying overnight bags and talking excitedly amongst themselves, stopped on the spot shocked. Security started running. 'Oohs' and 'Awws' were heard across the parking lot.

"Hank. Answer me now." Ms. Edison tried to yell above the noise. She was responsible for all the students on the field trip.

"They've decided to stay aboard." Hank tried to shout back at her.

"Travis, his Mom, Tara, and Luci - they've joined the Hovership, and I hope..." Hank was silent.

It was useless to try to explain. Ms. Edison couldn't hear above the noise. And there was nothing she could do. As the ship lifted, cords and steel lines ripped off the docking station. Loose electrical wires sparked as they hit against the parking lot, creating a monstrous looking creature. Utility pipes spouting water whipped and splashed around snapping wires. It was like the earth was gnashing at the hovering ship, demanding that it return.

Hank and his classmates watched it lift off in excitement and awe. They could hear sirens from across Tampa headed their way. On the bridge in the distance, Hank could see flashing red and blue lights. For a second, he turned to share this spectacle with Travis and Luci, forgetting they weren't there. It felt like a piece of him was missing. He was alone, even in the crowd of his classmates, clapping gleefully. He wasn't sure he would ever get over this feeling.

As the buzzing got louder, the Hovership lifted, blocking out a disc sized chunk of stars. The whole parking lot seemed to erupt in chaos. Parkers and students were hooting and hollering, not sure what was happening, but glad to be part of the party. The students on the busses were hanging out the windows to get a better look. At Hank's side, Ms. Edison was shouting, holding her head, pained. The other chaperones and teachers were standing, mouths open. Hank's stomach heaved in response, but it did that often these days. He was scared to be in the know and lost in the knowledge that he was left. Despite these protests, the glowing green shadow of the ship headed out to the gulf. Hank watched it slip into the horizon, a thin line of blinking lights following the path of the moon. His eyes glazed over as he held his last toggle. And he wondered.

The End

Acknowledgements

This book is dedicated to the memory of my father, Kenneth McCoy Drummond who died unexpectedly shortly after it was completed. He never got to read it, but he supported me and unknowingly helped me see it through to the end. He taught me to always learn and wonder about the world, a gift I will cherish for the rest of my life.

There are many others to whom I am indebted. Thank you to all the people who read even a portion of the earlier drafts. I owe the world to my family, who gave me a home during the recession where I could write and live. To my friends, old and new, who have always been a great joy and encouraged me to laugh. Special thanks to Kara, Cassandra and Taft who kept me going during the doubtful days. Sara's teachers, friends and their families inspired us during very tough times. Annette, you reminded me to have confidence when I needed it. If you find your name randomly in Dr. Wren's world – please do not wonder at the reference, good or bad - this is a work of fiction and it was merely a nod in your honor. If you don't find your name, I have two more books to go. I am grateful and humbled by all your support.

About the Author

SHELLY DRUMMOND IS A FOLKLORIST and retired archaeologist living in Plant City, Florida with her Mom, daughter and a dog that looks like Toto. Her short stories have been published in Blood and Aphorisms, Caution! and Broken Pencil magazines. She still hates ticks.